MOB
Princess
Count Your Blessings

Mob Princess

For Money and Love
Stolen Kisses, Secrets, and Lies

Also by Todd Strasser

How I Spent My Last Night on Earth
How I Created My Perfect Prom Date
How I Changed My Life
Shirt and Shoes Not Required
Boot Camp
Can't Get There from Here
Give a Boy a Gun
The DriftX series
The Impact Zone series

MOB
Princess
Count Your Blessings

TODD STRASSER

Simon Pulse

NEW YORK   LONDON   TORONTO   SYDNEY

This book is a work of fiction. Any references to historical events, real people, or real locales are used fictitiously. Other names, characters, places, and incidents are the product of the author's imagination, and any resemblance to actual events or locales or persons, living or dead, is entirely coincidental.

SIMON PULSE
An imprint of Simon & Schuster Children's Publishing Division
1230 Avenue of the Americas, New York, NY 10020
Copyright © 2007 by Todd Strasser
SIMON PULSE and colophon are registered trademarks of
Simon & Schuster, Inc.
Designed by Mike Rosamilia
The text of this book was set in New Caledonia.
Manufactured in the United States of America
First Simon Pulse edition December 2007
2 4 6 8 10 9 7 5 3 1
Library of Congress Control Number 2007932619
ISBN-13: 978-1-4169-3542-1
ISBN-10: 1-4169-3542-8

TO LIA AND GEOFF, WITH LOVE

Count Your Blessings

1

WHAT'S WRONG, KATIE?" LEO SWEETS ASKED. They were in his Mercedes-Benz, on a highway, driving toward the Metro Correctional Facility in New York City, where Kate's father, Sonny Blessing, was being held. The summer sun glared off the highly polished black hood. The air conditioner hummed loudly. Kate was wearing sunglasses.

"Sorry?" Kate had been distracted, gazing at a convertible in the lane next to them with two bare-chested boys and two girls wearing bikini tops in the back squeezed in next to a couple of body boards and beach chairs.

"You looked like you was far away," Leo said. This was true. Kate had been imagining herself, carefree and happy, in the back seat of that car, on the way to the beach to lie in the sun and play in the waves.

"Sorry," Kate said.

"Don't be sorry," said Leo. "Want to talk?"

Kate looked across at Leo, a heavyset man who refused to

give up either candy or his stained old beige tracksuit. Of all the men in her father's "organization," he was her favorite, sweet and concerned and always thinking about others. More like an uncle. An uncle who was missing a few teeth.

"Is it that obvious?" Kate asked.

"Maybe not to everyone," Leo said as he drove. "But it is to me. Then again, I know you since you were a baby. Besides, it's okay. You're supposed to feel bad when your old man gets pinched by the feds."

Kate sighed sadly and nodded. A few days before, her father had been arrested by the FBI on an assortment of serious crimes, including racketeering, bribery, and wire fraud. It was the sort of thing that could get a daughter down.

"You scared?" Leo asked.

Kate nodded. She lifted her long black hair off her neck so her skin could cool. Ever since her mom, Amanda, had left Kate's father the previous winter, Sonny had been in a physical and emotional free-fall. Kate was worried that the prospect of a long jail sentence would break him. And what would that would mean for her, and her brother, and mother?

"Don't worry," Leo said. "We'll post his bail and get him out. Danny'll start filing motions. He's an expert at slowing down the judicial process. It'll be years before Sonny goes to trial. Your father could be an old man before he has to take the stand in court."

That sounded reassuring, but Kate's problems were like an onion. If she peeled that worry away, another became exposed.

"It's not just my dad," Kate said. "I mean, that's definitely the biggest problem. But there are other things. There's this guy." She paused, uncertain whether she wanted to continue. She'd never really confided in Leo before. At least, not about her personal guy problems. Then again, she was running out of people to confide in.

"Joe Blattaria's son?" Leo asked.

Kate tensed, then turned and stared at him. "No, but how did you know about Nick? Did someone say something?"

Leo shook his head. "No. I just keep my eyes and ears open."

Kate remained tense. If Leo had noticed, what about the others? Joe Blattaria was her father's mortal enemy. So fooling around with his son would be regarded as a huge betrayal. "Leo, you can't ever say anything to anyone. If any of the guys in the organization were to find out that I had anything to do with Nick Blattaria—"

"Hey, come on, kiddo, who're you talking to?" Leo said, almost sounding a little bit hurt.

Kate relaxed a little. Leo was right. He was one person she'd never have to worry about betraying her.

"Sorry," Kate apologized. "You just scared me for a second. No, it has nothing to do with Nick Blattaria. That's over."

"Good," Leo said. "I gotta admit, that had me worried. No matter what, it couldn't lead to anything good."

Kate gazed out the car's window again. They were going over a bridge. Leo was in the right lane, as usual, driving just below the speed limit. Ahead of them rose the New York City skyline, concrete, steel, and glass shimmering and rippling in the summer heat. Kate shifted uncomfortably in her seat. She knew she'd just lied about Nick, both to Leo and herself. She *wanted* it to be over between them. But it wasn't. Not by a long shot. She still had feelings for him. And no matter how hard she tried, she couldn't get rid of them.

"So, you were saying there's this guy?" Leo said.

"Another guy," Kate said. "His name's Teddy. I was at his house on Twelve Mile Island when the story of Dad's arrest hit the papers."

"Yeah? So?"

"Teddy's father read the paper first," Kate said. "He told Teddy, and Teddy told me. His father . . . well, his parents, actually . . . they . . ."

"Don't approve of their son dating a girl whose father got pinched by the feds for racketeering, counterfeiting, and various other mob-related activities?" Leo guessed.

"You got it," Kate said sadly.

Leo heaved a sigh. "Katie, I gotta tell you something. You've probably already figured it out, but just in case you ain't, you live in a different world than other kids. You may go to the same school as they do, and to the same parties . . . they may be your friends . . . but they ain't in the same solar system. And they never will be."

"So . . . I can only date someone from our solar system?" Kate asked.

"No," Leo said. "I ain't sayin' that. You can date anyone you want. But the person you wind up with . . . they're either gonna be from our world . . . or they're gonna have to be willing to join it. So you gotta ask yourself: Is this Teddy guy gonna join our world someday?"

She couldn't imagine Teddy doing that. He was so straight, and earnest, and honest. He came from a world of country clubs, and prep schools, and Ivy League colleges. It was impossible to imagine him joining the world of organized crime.

"And what would stop me from leaving our world?" Kate asked.

"Nothin', Katie," Leo said. "*You're* the only thing that would stop you from leaving it."

Kate gazed over at Leo. Under the stained tan tracksuit, his belly pressed against the bottom of the car's steering wheel. "You think I should?"

"I can't answer that, sweetheart," Leo said. "All I can tell you is that our world ain't like the old days. I ain't sure the organization means as much as it once did. Now that there's all these computers and all this Internet stuff, you don't have to leave home to make good money. You gotta be stupid to go out and rob a bank or knock over an armored truck these days. There are a thousand cons and scams you can do right in your own house. What good's an organization when no one has to leave their house?"

"So you're saying?" Kate said.

"I ain't sure what I'm saying," Leo said. "Maybe I was wrong before. Maybe it ain't a question of whether or not you want to leave the organization. Maybe the real question is, how much longer is there gonna be an organization for you to leave?"

They were entering the city now. Leo drove into the thick traffic, moving slowly along with the yellow cabs and grumbling buses. Kate gazed up at the sunlight glinting off the windows of the tall buildings. Leo's answer made things both simpler and more complicated. If this was the end of her father's organization, then she didn't have to worry about whether or not she would leave it. But she'd never known life without the organization there to protect and comfort her.

Kate gazed at the crowded city sidewalks and began to feel nervous again. The last time her father had gone to jail, she'd been too young to visit him. And he'd only been there a day before bail was posted and he was back out. A few months later the charges were dropped completely, so the case had never gone to trial.

This time was different. Her father was facing a major federal rap. In addition to the mob-related activities, there was also bribery of public officials and tax evasion. Judges often spoke of "throwing the book" at a criminal. But in Sonny's case, they could throw a whole library.

"Here we are," Leo said, and drove the Mercedes into an underground parking garage. From there, he and Kate walked a few blocks to the federal lockup. The midday summer heat was ferocious, the city air so hot, it was difficult to breathe. Leo had to stop several times just to catch his breath. His collar was dark with sweat.

"Leo, you okay?" Kate asked. The top of her head felt hot, and she wished she'd worn a hat.

"Must be this heat," Leo said, struggling to catch his breath and dabbing his forehead with a handkerchief. They stepped into the shade of a doorway and waited for him to catch his breath. It seemed to take a long time, and even in the shade the older man continued to perspire.

"You *sure* you're okay?" Kate asked.

"Hey, I'm an old man," Leo said. "Give me a break."

"You're not that old," Kate said.

"What do you know?" Leo said with a smile. "You're a kid. Come on, let's get out of this heat."

They started to walk again. The federal building where her father was being held looked like any other massive concrete government building, only grayer and dirtier. Inside, the air was surprisingly cold. Kate and Leo both went through a metal detector manned by several seriously bored-looking guards, and then took an elevator. When they got off they had to go through yet another metal detector, this one manned by more guards. From there they passed through two sets of heavily fortified metal doors. Compared to this, the Riverton town jail was a playpen.

"Visitors?" a guard in a blue uniform asked once they'd gone through the last of the fortified doors.

Leo and Kate said they were.

"Who're you here to see?" asked the guard.

"Sonny Blessing," said Kate.

The guard's eyebrows rose as if he was surprised. Kate wondered why. Surely her father wasn't the first, or only, mobster he'd ever seen. He asked Kate and Leo to sign in, and then pointed them toward a door.

"What was that about?" Kate asked Leo in a low voice as they walked toward the door.

"They hit your father with a pretty high bail," Leo answered. "That always impresses these guys. It means your old man's a big deal."

The visitor's room was divided in half by a wall of clear Plexiglas, with desks and chairs on both sides. On the desks were phones. On the visitor side of the Plexiglas a few women sat with phones pressed against their ears, speaking to men in orange jumpsuits on the inmate side.

"The phones ain't just so we can't have any physical contact with the inmates," Leo whispered in Kate's ear. "They're also so's the feds can listen in to everything they say."

Kate understood what that meant: She wasn't to say anything incriminating.

"And one other thing," Leo said. "I just want to warn you, Katie. Your father may be . . . well, kind of unhappy, if you know what I mean. He's facing some pretty serious charges. And the feds do their homework. You gotta figure they got plenty of evidence against him. We'll find a way around this case, but it won't be easy. In the meantime, it's important to be upbeat. Encouraging. Know what I mean?"

"Understood," Kate said, taking a seat at a desk.

Leo pulled another chair beside hers and sat. Up close, the Plexiglas was smudged and scratched. They didn't wait long before a door opened and a prisoner came out, accompanied by a guard. Like the other inmates, he was wearing an orange jump-suit. On the back, in black block letters, it said FEDERAL BUREAU OF PRISONS. His hands were cuffed in front of him. He was bent, unshaven, and had a despondent, hopeless expression on his face. Almost like someone who'd given up the will to live. Kate glanced at him, looked away, then did a double take.

It was her father, Sonny.

2

KATE WAS SHOCKED. LEO HAD WARNED HER THAT HER
father might look unhappy, but she hadn't expected him
to look like a zombie. Her father glanced through the
Plexiglas, but when he saw his daughter and Leo, he didn't react.
Despite what Leo had said, Kate was surprised to see her father
looking so wretched and despondent.

The guard directed him to the desk. From his gaunt cheeks
Kate could tell that he'd lost weight. Sonny sat down but made no
effort to pick up the phone. Instead, he merely stared through
the Plexiglas, almost as if he didn't recognize his daughter on the
other side.

Leo nudged Kate to pick up her phone. With his hands still
cuffed together, Sonny picked up his. She cleaned the receiver
down with a wipe from a packet she always carried in her bag.

"Hi, Dad," she said, trying to be cheerful but not over the
top. No daughter wanted to appear happy about seeing her
father in jail.

"Hi, kid," Sonny answered glumly.

"Can't they uncuff you?" Kate asked. "That looks uncomfortable."

Sonny slowly shook his head. "Out of the cell, into the cuffs. That's the rule."

"So, you look a little thin," Kate said. "Are you feeling okay?

"The food's crap," her father grunted.

Kate waited for him to say something more. When he didn't, she told him that she and her brother were doing fine. She wasn't sure whether asking how he was would be a good idea. It was pretty obvious that things were bad.

"Guess there's not a lot to say, huh?" Sonny said.

"Things'll get better, Dad," Kate said.

"Oh, yeah?" Sonny asked dubiously, and raised an eyebrow. "How's that? I'm never gonna get out of here. Even if I get out, our operation's still shut down. There'll be no money coming in. Maybe I should count my blessings. At least in here, I got a roof over my head and three crummy meals a day."

Kate felt her insides twist uncomfortably. Their main source of income had been the factory, and that was shut down, but there was still her new venture with her best friend, Randi Stone, which involved producing and selling high-quality phony driver's licenses. True, it was still making pennies compared to what her father's organization was used to making, but at least it was something hopeful. But here in the federal lockup, and on these phones, there was no way she could tell her father about that.

Leo tapped gently on Kate's arm. "Ask him what the deal is."

Kate scowled, not understanding.

"He'll know what I mean," Leo said. "When it's a federal pinch, there's always a deal."

"Dad, Leo asked what the deal is," Kate said into the phone. "He said you'd know what he meant."

"Witness protection," Sonny answered.

Even Kate understood that answer. The feds were offering her father his freedom and a new identity in return for testifying against other members of his own organization as well as members of rival organizations. And, in this case, it would also include members of the Riverton police force who'd accepted bribes from her father's organization, and various members of the Blattaria organization, possibly including Nick. But to Kate, witness protection meant much more than that. It meant that she, her brother, and mother would also have to change their identities and move to someplace far away where nobody knew who they were. Kate wouldn't just lose her name and address. She'd lose Nick, Teddy, and her friends.

The door behind Sonny opened and a huge, tattooed man in the orange jumpsuit entered the inmate side of the room. He took a seat at the desk next to her father. On Kate's side of the Plexiglas a small, birdlike woman in extremely tight jeans sat down to speak with him.

"Where were you?" Sonny asked on the telephone on the other side of the smudged, scratched Plexiglas.

"Sorry?" Kate said. She'd been momentarily distracted by the huge man and tiny woman.

"When the FBI picked me up, you weren't home," her father said.

"You told me to stay away," Kate said.

"I know," said her father. "So, I was just wondering where were you?"

"I was with a friend," Kate said.

"A boyfriend?" Sonny asked.

This line of questioning caught Kate by surprise. It seemed unimportant compared to everything else that was going on in their lives. "Dad, why do you want to know?" she asked uncomfortably. Her father didn't know about Teddy, whose wealthy parents were pillars of the local community.

"Not Nick Blattaria, right?" her father said.

"No, I wasn't with Nick," said Kate.

That should have been the end of his questions, so she was surprised when Sonny said, "Then who?"

"Dad, I don't see how that could matter," Kate said.

Sonny leveled his gaze at her. He wedged the phone against his ear with his shoulder and drummed the desktop with his fingers. Kate knew it was a sign that he couldn't explain why he wanted to know. Not when the feds were listening to these phones.

"He's just a guy I know," Kate said.

Her father raised an eyebrow but said nothing, inviting her to continue.

"His name's Teddy Fitzgerald, and he's a friend from school," Kate said.

"What business is his father in?" Sonny asked.

"Dad, seriously, why the questions?" Kate asked uncomfortably. It wasn't that she was worried about what the feds might overhear. Clearly, Teddy and his family had nothing to hide. She just wasn't used to her father being so nosy about her personal life.

Her father kept drumming the desktop with his fingers. He was waiting for her answer.

"Some kind of banking business," Kate said. "Hedge funds. They're very rich."

The whole topic of Teddy was upsetting. Not just because, at Teddy's beach house two days before, it was his father who had found the newspaper article about Sonny being arrested by the FBI. And not just because the Fitzgeralds had made it obvious that they wanted Kate to leave the beach house immediately. But because she'd been unable to reach Teddy by phone, text, IM, or e-mail since.

Sonny nodded, apparently satisfied with her answer. He moved on to another subject: "You watching the house?"

"I've been staying there," Kate said.

"Where's Sonny Junior been staying?" her father asked.

"He's been staying with Mom, but I think he's coming back tonight."

"You're gonna be there, right?" her father said. "I don't want him staying in the house alone."

"I'll be there," Kate said.

Sonny was quiet for a moment. He glanced at Leo, then back at Kate. "Tell Leo you and I need to speak in private."

Kate turned to Leo and told him. The older man got up and crossed the room and stood near the guard.

"Now that I'm not there, you gotta take care of certain things," Sonny said.

Kate widened her eyes as if reminding him that they weren't on a private line. Her father nodded back to say he was aware of that. "The lawn's got to be watered," he said.

Kate nodded. They both knew the lawn was watered by an automatic sprinkler system.

"Make sure you skim the pool," he said.

"Right," said Kate, knowing the pool had built-in skimmers.

"Defrost the freezer," Sonny said.

Kate stared at him uncertainly through the Plexiglas.

"Not the one in the kitchen," Sonny said. "The one out in the garage."

"Gotcha." Kate nodded. Her father had just told her there was something in the freezer in the garage he wanted her to find.

"Now when Sonny Junior comes to stay with you, I don't want you eating junk," Sonny went on. "I want you to make sure you eat well. Some protein at every meal. And I want you and Sonny Junior to make sure you're getting enough vegetables. You can use up the frozen ones first."

"The ones in the freezer?" Kate said.

For the first time, Sonny smiled. That was the message. Whatever he wanted her to get from the freezer was hidden in a box of vegetables.

Now it was Kate's turn to ask questions. "Dad, how long . . . do you think you're going to be in here?"

The smile disappeared from her father's face. "You got ten million bucks?"

Kate blinked in astonishment. *Bail was ten million?* No wonder the guard had given her that look. "Not with me," she replied with a bittersweet smile.

"Danny's gonna try to talk them down," her father said.

Kate frowned, then gestured at the phone and her ear. Once again she wanted to make sure her father remembered that the feds listened in on these conversations.

Sonny shrugged. "It's what defense lawyers always try to do. That's no secret."

Wonderful, Kate thought bitterly. Maybe Danny could get the bail down to eight million. What difference would it make?

"So that's the story, kid," Sonny said. "Until someone gets the bail lowered, this is where you'll find me."

The visit ended and Kate blew her father a kiss good-bye. Sonny returned a bittersweet smirk. It wasn't easy to be cheerful in the face of such daunting news. Her father appeared to have only two choices: Betray everyone he knew, or spend the rest of his life in prison.

A little while later, outside again in the white-hot summer heat, Kate and Leo walked down the sidewalk back to the parking garage.

"Leo, tell me if I'm wrong," Kate said, "but to me, it looks like unless one of us trips over the pot of gold at the end of the rainbow, my father is going to be in prison for a long time, no matter how many motions Danny files. It's not going to make a difference because we can't post bail."

Leo dabbed the sweat from his forehead with a handkerchief. "That about sums it up, Katie. I had no idea they were gonna slap him with that much bail. It's pretty obvious they have no intention of letting him go until he talks."

"Which means the witness protection program," Kate said. "But what happens to you?"

Leo flopped his hands helplessly at his sides. "What choice do I have? Who's gonna take care of Darlene? Your father goes witness protection, then I gotta go also."

Darlene was Leo's wife. She suffered from diabetes, hypertension, high blood pressure, and about forty other maladies.

"They'll do that?" Kate asked, surprised. "They'll put you in the witness protection program also?"

"Sure, why not?" Leo said. "What good would it do to put an old man like me in jail? Besides, these days it costs the prison system seventy, eighty thousand a year to keep a guy behind bars. They don't want to spend that on someone harmless like me."

"But, that's good news, isn't it?" Kate said. "I mean, it's a pain to have to change your identity and move, but at least you won't be in jail."

Leo shook his head. "It's the worst thing they could do to me. They put me in the program, there goes my plans for retiring to Florida to be near my grandkids."

"Why?"

"'Cause that's the deal with witness protection," Leo said. "They can't put you anywhere near a place where it would be obvious you'd want to go. Everyone knows I want to be near my kids and grandchildren. I testify and then disappear, that's the first place my enemies are gonna look."

The implications came together in Kate's head. "So . . . the only way you get to retire and be near your grandchildren is if my father stays in jail and doesn't talk?"

Leo gave her a long, sad look. "Pretty crappy choice, huh? What's best for him is what's worst for me, and vice versa."

"If you were him, what would you do?" Kate asked.

"I'd talk," Leo said.

Kate grimaced.

"Come on, Katie," Leo said. "You want him to spend the rest of his life in jail? You want him to die there?"

"But you and he have been like brothers," Kate said.

"Doesn't matter," Leo said. "The whole code of silence thing went out with cement shoes. These days, it's every man for himself."

They got the car and started to drive back to Riverton. The traffic leaving the city at that time of day was light. Kate recalled those guys and girls in that convertible. By now they were surely at the beach, having the kind of carefree fun she could only fantasize about. Meanwhile, in the driver's seat, Leo was silent and glum.

"Thinking about the grandchildren?" Kate asked.

Leo nodded. "It's gonna break Darlene's heart."

Kate didn't know what to say. She'd never imagined that things would get so bad that her father would be faced with such terrible choices. On the highway, Leo switched lanes. Kate glanced into the side-view mirror just in time to the see a familiar-looking red minivan a couple of cars back switch lanes to stay behind them.

"Leo, get in the left lane and hit the gas," Kate said.

Leo frowned and looked into the rearview mirror. "We got company?"

"I think so, but I'll know for sure in a second," Kate said.

Leo hit the gas, and the Mercedes took off. Behind them, the red minivan weaved in and out of lanes, trying to keep up without being obvious about it. It had to be the feds.

"I don't get it," Kate said. "I thought they'd gotten what they want."

"Can I slow down now?" Leo asked. He was bent forward and clutching the steering wheel tightly, obviously uncomfortable going over the speed limit.

"Sure."

"Thanks." Leo slowed down and got back into the right lane. Three cars back, the red minivan also settled into the right lane.

Kate couldn't imagine why the FBI was still doing undercover surveillance. They'd gotten her father. There was no one higher up in the organization to get.

"So, Katie, I gotta ask you a question," Leo said. "Now that we know what we know, what are we gonna do? I mean in terms of the organization. It ain't completely dead yet, you know. We still got the sports-betting operation and the Internet scams. And we got guys who need to make a living, you know?"

Kate knew this was no small question. It was probably the biggest thing she'd ever been asked. Her family ran the Blessing organization. Or, at least, they ran what was *left* of it. And with her father in jail and her mother out of the picture, whatever responsibility remained fell on Kate's shoulders.

But Kate suspected that wasn't the only reason Leo had asked what she wanted to do. Over the past six months Kate had proven that she could be a leader. She had handled the men in the organization numerous times, given them orders, solved problems, and even stood up to Uncle Benny Hacksaw, the craziest, most vicious member of the crew. At first she'd surprised even herself by how well she'd done. But then she'd realized that the men wanted to be told what to do. They needed structure and guidance. The Blessing organization may have been underworld, but it required the same management style as any other company: organization, discipline, and positive reinforcement. Everything she'd learned about in the FBLA—Future Business Leaders of America. Leo gave Kate a sideways glance. She knew he was waiting for her answer.

"My father's going to keep running the organization," Kate replied.

Leo's forehead bunched. "I know guys have run organizations from the slammer before, Katie. But I don't think your father's in any shape to do that."

"I don't either," Kate agreed. "So our job will be to make everyone *think* my father's in shape to do it."

"Yeah, but who'll really be in charge?" Leo asked.

"The two people in the black Mercedes in the right lane doing fifty miles an hour in the fifty-five-mile-an-hour zone," Kate said.

Leo frowned. "Us?"

"We've pretty much been doing it for the last six months, Leo," Kate said. "There's no reason to stop now."

"But that was different, Katie," Leo said. "At least your father was around some of the time."

He was right, of course. It would be different. And harder. But still, she'd done it before. Maybe she could do it again. What choice did she have?

3

LEO PULLED UP TO HER HOUSE. "YOU GONNA BE okay here by yourself?"

Kate glanced at the naked-lady fountain in the middle of the circular driveway. The fountain had stopped working, and the water around it had turned green. Dead leaves floated on it. All around the house things had gotten really run down. "I'll be okay."

"You sure?" Leo asked.

No, Kate wasn't sure, but what good would saying that do? "You're sweet, Leo, but I'll be fine." She leaned over and kissed him on the cheek, then got out.

Outside the car, the heat literally took her breath away. The best place to spend the rest of the day would be by the pool, but first she had some things to do.

She went into the house, then through the kitchen to the garage. Her father's black BMW and her red Mercedes were parked there, along with a trail bike Sonny Jr. had used once and fallen off of. In the back of the garage was an old freezer where they kept extra food. Kate could remember times when—after her father's crew had hijacked a truck—it had been filled to the top with frozen meats. But now, when she opened it, it was less than a third full, and what was in there was covered by thick white frost. Given the heat of the day, Kate welcomed reaching down into the chilly depths, feeling the cold air against her face. She pushed aside some frozen steaks and ice-cream containers. Under a frozen pizza she found a box of broccoli covered with a layer of white frost. Kate closed the freezer and went into the kitchen.

The box looked perfectly normal and was sealed. For a few moments while she ran it under luke warm water in the sink, Kate wondered if all she was doing was defrosting some perfectly good broccoli. When the packaging became soggy, she started to unwrap it. Inside was a waxy white lining, and when it was peeled away, Kate found herself holding a block of green inside a Ziploc plastic bag—neat wads of hundred-dollar bills with rubber bands around them.

Kate took the bag of money up to her room. She wanted to see if there was anything on MySpace from Teddy. As she climbed the wide marble staircase, she warned herself not to be disappointed if he hadn't written. She couldn't actually remember seeing a computer at the beach house, although she would have been very surprised if the Fitzgeralds didn't have several. But the warning made no difference. She knew she would be disappointed. Seriously so. Yes, it was true that the news of her father's arrest had come as a terrible shock on Saturday morning, but what about the night before that, when Teddy had held her in his arms and made love to her? He couldn't have forgotten about that. She sure hadn't forgotten.

Perhaps to some girls, sex was no big thing.

But it was to Kate.

She tossed the plastic bag of money on the bed and sat down at the computer. There had to be a message from Teddy. There just *had* to be.

Because if there wasn't, it wouldn't *just* be that Teddy had let her down. It would be the same exact thing that had happened to her with Nick six months ago.

A wonderful night of lovemaking.

Followed by an unexpected separation in the morning.

Followed by days and days of waiting for a message that never came.

Kate wasn't ready to go through that again.

Her MySpace page came on the screen. Kate felt her hopes vaporize into nothingness, and her mood turn dark. There were two messages from Randi, but none from Teddy.

This can't happen again, she thought miserably. *It just can't.* She could feel the tears that wanted to well up in her eyes and spill out. So let them, she thought. She was alone. What did it matter? But there was another part of her. An angry part. And that part said no. She was fed up with this crap from guys. Why should she let them hurt her like this?

To distract herself, Kate turned to the e-mails from Randi.

The first had been copied to a long list of other addresses and contained an attachment labeled "What You Didn't Know About Stu McLean and Tanner Westfall."

Despite her anger, Kate felt herself begin to smile even before she'd opened the attachment. This video was revenge for a video Stu and Tanner had distributed of Randi in a "compromised position" at Kate's New Year's Eve party the previous winter. To get back at them, Randi had hidden a camera in Teddy's pool house at the beach. The video clip was a montage of shots: Stu and Tanner in the Fitzgeralds' pool house pulling off their board shorts, coming out of a shower, toweling off. Randi had edited it so that no one would suspect that they'd just come from the cold ocean and had taken cold showers. But the bodily evidence was unmistakable.

Kate laughed out loud. After the nasty rumors Tanner had spread about her the previous winter when she broke up with him, and the video Stu had made of Randi, this revenge tasted very sweet.

The second e-mail from Randi invited Kate to an outdoor concert that night at the park.

From downstairs came a beep that meant someone had come through the driveway gate. It was hard for Kate to imagine who that could possibly be. By the time she got downstairs, her mother's Mercedes had stopped outside and Kate could hear keys jingling as her mother searched for the right one to let herself into the house.

Kate was filled with sudden hope. Was her mother coming

home now that Kate's father was about to experience an extended stay in prison? She pulled open the door. Amanda was standing outside in white capris and a slinky, low-cut teal blue top. In her hand was a key fob filled with keys.

"Ah!" Amanda jumped back with surprise when the door suddenly opened. The keys clattered to the ground.

"How soon they forget," Kate said, bending down and picking up the keys.

"Meaning?" Her mother said, pressing her hand against her chest as if to hide her rapidly beating heart.

Kate gestured at the keys. "Meaning you've only been gone half a year and already you can't remember which keys go where?"

The corners of her mother's mouth dropped. "And it's so good to see you, too. Now how about giving your mother a break, okay?" She came into the house and stood on the black marble floor of the foyer, looking around. Brown, wilted, dead flowers sagged over the sides of vases, pictures on the walls hung askew, and sizable dust balls hugged the corners. "What happened here?"

"I told you the place was falling apart without you," Kate said.

"I thought you were just trying to guilt-trip me," Amanda said. "Wasn't anyone capable of picking up a phone and calling a cleaning service?"

Kate decided to skip the banter and cut to the chase. "Are you here because you've decided to come home?"

Amanda's shoulders sloped downward. "I'm sorry, hon. I just

came by to get some summer things." She started up the marble stairs. Kate followed.

"I assume you do know about Dad," Kate said. Now that her mother was hanging out with Marvin the dentist and the rest of the country club set, there was a slight chance she might have missed the news.

"Yes." Amanda nodded. "It's really a shame, but I guess it was bound to happen sooner or later. Thank God he's got Danny. I've never known a lawyer who has as many tricks up his sleeve."

"Not this time, Mom," Kate said.

Her mother stopped on the stairs and looked back at her with a frown.

"Bail's been set at ten million," Kate explained.

Amanda's eyes widened with surprise. "That's ridiculous! Can't Danny get it down?"

"Suppose he got them to cut it in half," Kate said. "What difference would it make? Know anyone with an extra five million?"

Amanda pursed her lips. "Good point. Well, I'm sorry to hear about that." She started up the stairs again. "Especially as it will affect you and Sonny Junior."

"So, if we know Dad probably isn't coming home anytime soon," Kate said, following her mother into the bedroom, "then why won't you come home? It's not like you'll have to worry about running in to him."

In her bedroom, Amanda turned on the light in the walk-in closet and went in. Ostensibly to get clothes but, Kate suspected, also to hide from her daughter.

"Mom?" Kate said, waiting outside the closet. She couldn't see her mother, but she could hear the rustling of clothes and the rattle of hangers.

"Kate, hon, think about it for a moment," her mother said.

"What's to think about?" Kate asked. "Dad's not here, so you can come home. The place obviously needs it, and it would be good for Sonny Junior, too. I really don't see what the problem is."

"You're not thinking of all the people involved," her mother said.

Kate thought. The realization came with a jolt. "You can't move back because of the dentist?"

"His name is Marvin," Amanda said. "And I don't think he'd feel very comfortable here."

"He's *living* with you?" Kate asked.

"We see a lot of each other," her mother said, coming out of the closet with some summer skirts and blouses.

"Mom, how serious is this?" Kate asked.

"Marvin thinks it's very serious," Amanda said. "I'm not sure yet." Having collected an armful of clothes, she started out of the bedroom. Kate followed.

"Mom, has it occurred to you that you're still married?" Kate asked. "And that the man you're married to is in serious trouble?"

"The man I'm married to decided a long time ago that it wasn't important to be faithful to his wife," Amanda replied as she headed down the stairs.

"So this is about revenge?" Kate asked. "That's all you can think about? You're just going to desert him in his hour of need?"

Amanda stopped on the stairs and glared back up at her daughter. "Would you please stop trying to guilt-trip me?" she asked sharply. "If I had a dollar for every night he didn't come home, and didn't call, and wasn't there for me in *my* hour of need, I'd probably be able to post his bail. Now I'm sorry about your father, I really am. And if I happened to have an extra ten million dollars lying around in a drawer somewhere, I would certainly post his bail for the sake of you and Sonny Junior. But your father made his bed a long time ago, and now he's going to have to lie in it."

Kate's mother turned and headed down the stairs once again with Kate following.

"But think about it, Mom. Dad's in jail because of certain activities that you benefited from greatly," Kate said. "Think of all the money he made and how well you've lived."

"I took care of his children," Amanda said. "I took care of his house. I helped him run his operations. Whatever I got out of the marriage, I earned."

They went out the front door to the car. Kate's mother stumbled, and several blouses fell to the ground. Kate picked them up and helped Amanda put the clothes in the backseat. When they'd finished, her mother turned to her with tears in her eyes. Amanda looked miserable, torn, and guilt-ridden.

Kate put her arms around her and hugged her. "I'm sorry, Mom. You're right. You didn't know the feds were going to grab him. You didn't know this was coming. You have a right to take care of yourself. It's just bad timing, that's all."

At that, Amanda burst into tears.

"Mom, what's wrong?" Kate asked, confused by Amanda's reaction.

Amanda shook her head and dug tissues out of her bag and blew her nose. Her eyes were almost raccoon-like with smudged mascara.

"Really, Mom, what is it?" Kate asked.

"It's worse when you act like you understand," her mother said with a sniff.

"Why?" Kate asked, completely bewildered.

"I can't explain it. Someday you'll understand." Amanda dabbed her eyes and looked at the house. Her gaze drifted over to the naked-lady fountain and the murky green water around it. "I don't want you staying here alone."

"Where would you suggest I go?" Kate asked.

"You could stay with Leo and Darlene," Amanda said. "They'd be happy to have you. And now that all their kids have moved out, they've got the room."

This was true. But what would it mean for her father's organization? This house had always been the headquarters, the refuge, the symbol of the Blessing organization's prosperity. If they abandoned it, what message did that send to the men in the organization? What message did that send to the Blattarias, who were so determined to take over her father's territory?

"I'm not going," Kate said. "I'm staying here."

Her mother gave her an uncertain look. "Why?"

"Because I'm not giving up on this organization," Kate said. "I have to keep it going for Dad's sake, for my sake, and for the men. If I walk out of this house, it sends the wrong message. So I'm not going to do that."

Her mother's forehead wrinkled. "Whose idea is this?"

"Mine," Kate said.

Amanda smiled knowingly. The way she'd smiled the time Sonny Jr. was nine years old and said he was going to run away forever and she'd said, "You go right ahead, just be home for dinner."

"No offense or anything, Mom, but you don't know what's been going on for the past six months," Kate said. "I wouldn't say I've been running the organization for Dad, but I've been helping a lot."

The smile vanished from her mother's face. "You realize there's a huge difference between helping and leading, don't you? When your father was around, even if he wasn't functioning well, he was still a presence to be reckoned with. Now that he's behind bars, it's going to be very different. These are macho men, Kate. Half of them are probably complete misogynists. They're not going to take kindly to a seventeen-year-old girl telling them what to do. So let's be sensible about this. Pack up the things you need. I'll call Leo and Darlene. You know how they both adore you—"

"No," Kate said firmly. "You've made your choice; I've made mine. I'm staying here."

"You can't," Amanda said. "Not alone. . . ."

But Kate made no sign of changing her mind. Her mother

may have left her father, but Kate was here to stay.

Amanda gazed at her with a slightly astonished expression. "You've changed."

The words caught Kate by surprise as she realized that, through her mother's eyes, this was true. She's been hurt and disappointed by the only two guys she'd ever really cared about. And that had made her realize how important family was. *They* were the only ones you really could depend on. But it cut both ways: If she wanted to be able to depend on her family, then they had to be able to depend on her. Right now, her father needed her, and she wasn't going to let him down.

"I'll be okay here by myself," Kate said. "I've got your number and Leo's number and the crew's. I know if I need anyone, they're only a phone call away."

Her mother's expression changed from astonishment to uncertainty. "What about money?"

"Not a problem," Kate said. "At least, for now."

"I don't know about this," Amanda said. But even as she spoke, she was moving around to the driver's side of the car.

"It's going to be okay, Mom, really," Kate assured her.

"Promise you'll call?" her mother said, opening the door.

"Promise," Kate said.

They blew kisses to each other, and then Amanda got into her car and drove around the circle and back down the driveway. Kate stood in the doorway and watched until the car disappeared. Then she closed the door and leaned with her back against it and looked around the foyer. It wasn't like this would be the first night she'd ever spent alone in the house. She'd done it plenty of times.

The difference was, this would be the first time she would spend it alone, knowing that there was no chance of her father coming home.

4

RANDI INSISTED ON PICKING HER UP THAT NIGHT ON THE way to the concert. Kate didn't understand why. Usually, when they went somewhere together, they took Kate's car. Still, if that's what Randi wanted, she wasn't going to argue.

In the meantime, Kate got ready to go out. As she got dressed, she had one eye on the mirror and the other on the computer, still hoping a message from Teddy would pop up. It distressed her that he'd made no effort to contact her. He had to know how upsetting it had been to be asked to leave his parents' house. She knew he cared deeply about her. Their last night together hadn't been about sex. It had been the culmination of months of growing closer, enjoying each other's company, and learning about each other's lives. Had it not been for her unfortunate "detour" with Nick, it probably would have all happened much sooner.

But now that it had happened, she wanted to hear from Teddy. She *needed* to hear from him. She couldn't understand why she *hadn't* heard from him.

Kate continued to try on clothes, trying to decide what to wear that night. Some sense of survival was urging her to look hot. To go out and strut her stuff and turn heads to reassure herself that Nick Blattaria and Teddy Fitzgerald were not the only two guys in the world. And that if, God forbid, Teddy let her down the way Nick had, she was still an attractive young woman who could have her pick of men.

Not that she wanted someone new right now. That was the farthest thing from her mind. Mostly she just wanted to feel good about herself.

By now, there was a pile of clothes on Kate's bed. Somewhere near the bottom was a pair of jeans she'd tried on, then rejected. But now she was thinking that maybe she should try them again. She dug down through the clothes on the bed and found the jeans and the Ziploc bag filled with hundred-dollar bills.

Kate couldn't help smiling to herself. She'd been so lost in thought about her personal problems that she'd forgotten about the money. She was glad it was there. There was still at least one man she could count on: her father.

She heard a buzz from downstairs and knew that Randi was at the gate. She quickly pulled on the jeans and ran downstairs to let her in. Fortunately she was already wearing a top she liked and had done her hair and makeup. She went out the front door and was caught by surprise when Randi drove up in a hot little black Lexus IS 300. Now Kate understood why Randi wanted to drive that night.

"Wait a minute," she said, stepping out into the dark. "Last week you were driving a Toyota Corolla."

"I took it back to the dealer," Randi said, getting out. "It wasn't me."

The Lexus wasn't the only thing that was different. Randi's hair looked fabulous, her new True Religion jeans couldn't have been hotter, and her necklace sparkled with gems.

"I thought the whole point of our new venture for you was to save money for college," Kate said.

"Get real, sweetheart," Randi said, putting her hand on her hip and giving her a coy look. "When we're making this kind of money, who needs college?"

"It's going that well?" Kate asked, surprised. Given the problems with her father lately, she hadn't been paying that much attention to their venture.

"Can you spell exponential?" Randi asked. "I can't, but it's a good thing I can count. I'd say it's going *extremely* well."

Kate was glad to hear it, even though she had a feeling that Randi's idea of what extremely well meant in terms of income was still far from where they needed to be. Her jeans might have been True Religion, but the Lexus was used and the glimmering stones in her necklace were no doubt cubic zirconia.

"Let's roll," Randi said, getting back into the Lexus. Kate got in. Randi turned on the AC and cranked up some hip-hop. "So I heard about your dad," she said as they drove out the driveway gate. "Bummer."

Kate nodded.

"What's it mean for you?" Randi asked.

"It means it's a good thing our new venture is paying off," Kate said.

"What about your mom?" Randi asked.

"She's got her own life to lead," Kate said.

"And Teddy?"

Kate raised her hands. "Do we have to?"

"No, sorry," Randi apologized. "I didn't mean to start interrogating you . . . but, I guess that means things aren't good?"

"His father found the story about my dad in the newspaper," Kate said. "I was at their beach house. It was very obvious they didn't want me there."

"*Teddy* didn't want you there?" Randi said.

"No, his parents," Kate said. Pride kept her from adding that while it had been his parents who had wanted her to leave, she still had not heard from Teddy himself.

"That must have sucked bigtime," Randi said. "But I thought Teddy was Mr. I-Don't-Care-What-My-Parents-Think."

"I guess we'll see about that," Kate said, eager to change the subject. "Anyway, what's the response been to the shrinkage video?"

Randi grinned broadly. "If I were those guys, I wouldn't be showing my face in public anytime soon."

The concert in the park that night was open-mike, dominated by local hip-hop bands with names like Ambiguous Genitalia and The Natural Ingredients. Crowds of kids danced in front of the band shell. The air was hot and humid, and the smell of barbecue was everywhere. In the Lexus, Randi and Kate cruised past the scene with the windows open.

"Looks like fun," Randi said.

Kate wanted to agree. She wanted to get out there and party and dance and have fun and try to pretend either that she'd heard from Teddy and everything was okay, or that she'd gotten past Teddy and was ready for someone new.

But the problem with pretending was that it was just pretend.

Randi kept driving. Parked cars lined both sides of the street and a PARKING LOT FULL sign blocked the entrance to the closest lot.

"We'll have to go to the next lot," Randi said. They drove about a quarter of a mile to the next parking lot and found a spot.

Kate and Randi got out. This parking lot was dark and almost quiet. The music from the concert was distant. There were lots of cars parked here, but hardly any people. Randi opened the Lexus's trunk. Inside was a Thermos from which she poured two Red Bulls and vodka into plastic cups. She raised her cup. "To continued health and prosperity."

And ten million miraculous dollars to get my dad out of jail, Kate thought.

The drink lifted Kate's spirits. With the music thumping in the distance, the idea of dancing out all her frustrations became very appealing. She and Randi finished their drinks, then started to wind their way through the parked cars and toward the road that led to the band shell.

"Well, well, what are the chances of this?" a voice said from out of nowhere.

Kate squinted into the dark. A group of people were walking toward them. Suddenly she realized they were Tanner, Stu, and the three girls they called the BMWs—Brandy Burton, Mandy Mannis, and Wendy Williams—otherwise known as Blond, Blonder, and Blondest. All of them were carrying beers.

Randi stopped and looked around nervously as if for an escape route.

"Looking for something?" Stu asked as he and the others came closer.

He was walking unsteadily and slurring his words, a sure sign that he'd already had a lot to drink.

Next to Kate, Randi took a deep breath to calm her nerves and faced him. "Look, an eye for an eye, okay? If you can't take it, you shouldn't have dished it out."

Stu glanced at Kate and then said to Randi, "I wouldn't be walking around in dark parking lots if I were you."

"Are you threatening her?" Kate asked, feeling her ire grow.

"I'm just saying people have been known to get hurt," Stu said.

"Don't be stupid," Kate said.

"Stay out of this, Kate," Stu said.

"It's not like you could do anything, anyway," Brandy Burton sneered. "Now that Daddy's gone bye-bye to the big house."

"Yeah, Kate," Tanner agreed. "And it's not like Randi could have pulled off her little cinematic stunt without some help from you." He turned to his friends. "You know last year when I dumped this chick I was actually scared her old man would send out his thugs to break my legs? Guess I won't have to worry about that anymore."

Kate snorted. "Aren't you the one who came crawling back on his hands and knees begging me to take you back?"

"Not likely." Tanner smirked, even though what Kate had said was true.

"So what happens now, Kate?" Mandy asked. "No more New Year's Eve pool parties? No more Fourth of July fireworks shows? The cute little red Benz gets repossessed? I hear your mom's already living in an apartment in town. Sounds like she got out just in the nick of time."

The digs dug deep. Kate felt her hands ball into fists.

Brandy swiveled her head as if she was looking for someone. "So where's Teddy Money Bags, anyway?" She dramatically brought her hands to her cheeks. "Oh, no! Now that daddy's in jail, don't tell me Kate's been dumped again!?"

It was a lucky guess, but right on target. The words stung worse than salt on an open wound.

"Too bad, Kate," said Mandy. "It must be tough when all the sugar daddies are gone."

Kate felt like she was going to explode. The nerve of these three girls, who had to be the most spoiled brats in all of Riverton. "Looks who's talking!" Kate sputtered. "The three of you wouldn't have anything if it weren't for your rich parents."

"At least our parents have *legitimate* jobs," Brandy said, actually sticking her nose up in the air.

Kate's fuse was burning down quickly. As if her life wasn't already difficult enough, she didn't need this chorus of jerks making it worse. She'd had it with trying to be nice. If these lameoids wanted to dish, she'd show them dishing like—suddenly she felt Randi's hand close gently but firmly on her arm. "Come on, Kate, let the piranhas find a cow carcass to gnaw on."

"What?" said Wendy.

"It's a metaphor," Randi explained.

Wendy looked mystified.

"See, piranhas are these vicious fish that can rip all the flesh off a cow in minutes," Randi started to explain.

"I wouldn't eat a cow carcass," Wendy said.

"You've never had a hamburger?" Randi asked.

"That's different," Wendy said.

Even Tanner groaned at that. Meanwhile, Brandy shot Randi an appraising look. "Well, well, check out the hair and jeans and that Lexus. Only, aren't you the girl whose father's music store just went out of business?"

"Oh, I know!" said Mandy. "*That's* why they're friends. They both have loser fathers."

Brandy wasn't finished with Randi. "So fess up, girl. What's with the hot car and fancy threads?"

"Back off," Kate snarled.

"Or what?" Brandy asked with a haughty laugh. "Gonna sic Daddy on us? Oh, wait! Daddy's getting his clothes pressed in the prison laundry."

That one tipped Kate over the edge. She let her anger get the best of her. "My father has friends, you know. And they're *not* in jail."

The small crowd of taunters actually quieted while they considered that.

"So?" Brandy scoffed. "Like they might ever listen to *you*?"

"Yeah, we're sooo scared." Mandy grinned.

A pair of headlights swung on them. The group squinted at the car. Kate spotted the rack of lights.

"The cops!" Tanner hissed.

Kate heard beer cans clatter on the asphalt. At the same time, she felt Randi pull her away. With Stu, Tanner, and the BMWs suddenly preoccupied, it was the right moment to leave.

Kate and Randi walked out to the road and headed toward the concert.

"You can't let them get to you," Randi said.

"Easier said than done," Kate grumbled.

"You just have to remind yourself that they don't matter," Randi counseled. "One more year and you'll never have to see any of them again, if you don't want to. Or you can come back to the twenty-fifth reunion and enjoy what they've become. Mandy will weigh two hundred pounds, and Stu will have a really bad comb-over."

Kate wished it were that easy. But it wasn't just Tanner, Stu, and the BMWs that were getting her down. It was them *and* everything else. Her father, Teddy, her future, her life. Kate stopped and looked back at the parking lot.

"What is it?" Randi asked.

"The Red Bull and vodka," Kate said.

"Forget it, Kate. Remember the police car?"

"We could wait until they go," Kate said.

"Oh, come on." Randi slid her arm through Kate's and kept

walking. "Why drown your sorrows when you can dance them away?"

Kate allowed herself to be led away, but she had her doubts that dancing alone could do the trick.

Half an hour later, that feeling had become a reality. Despite the music and plenty of guys, she just couldn't get in the mood. The worries weighed heavily on her, and trying to dance was like trying to do ballet while lifting weights. It was killing her that she still hadn't heard from Teddy. It made her wonder if there was something wrong with her, and she *hated* when she started to feel that way. Finally she turned to Randi and said she wanted to go home.

Like the good friend that she was, Randi didn't argue.

"Sorry, I didn't mean to ruin the fun," Kate said as they walked back toward the parking lot.

"It's okay," Randi said. "You tried."

"It's just a really bad time for me right now," Kate said.

"Anything I can do?" Randi asked.

Kate looked at her friend's new hair and new clothes. She thought about the sporty Lexus in the parking lot. "There is one thing," she said.

"I'm all ears," Randi said.

"I think we need to keep our new venture a little quieter," Kate said.

"I haven't told anyone except the boys," Randi said. The boys were their friends Shane Haslet and Adam Frost, who were assisting in their new venture.

"Sometimes we can say things without talking," Kate said.

Randi scowled for a moment, but then gave Kate an exaggerated nod. "Ah. In other words, I'm being too showy?"

"Maybe for the time being," Kate said. They reached the dark parking lot, and the Lexus came into view.

"I don't have to go back to the Toyota Corolla, do I?" Randi asked in a little-girl voice.

Despite the situation, Kate couldn't help chuckling. "I don't think so."

They were only a few blocks from Kate's house when she remembered the red minivan from the day she and Leo had gone to see her father in the federal lockup. Now that she thought of it, maybe it would be better if Randi didn't drive her all the way home. The last thing they needed was to have the FBI snooping around Randi.

"I think maybe you'd better drop me off and let me walk the rest of the way," Kate said.

"Why?" asked Randi.

"No logical reason," Kate said, not wanting to scare her friend. "Just playing it safe."

"You sure?" Randi asked.

Kate shook her head. "No, I'm not sure about anything. That's why I think we should play it safe for now. Okay?"

Randi slowed down. The street was dark here and lined with woods. The streetlights were far apart.

"You sure you want to walk in the dark?" Randi asked.

"I'll be careful," Kate said.

Randi brought the car to a stop and gazed uncertainly at Kate. "You know, there was one thing that idiot Mandy said."

"Loser fathers?" Kate guessed.

Randi nodded. "What a bitch."

Kate smiled bitterly. "Funny how the truth hurts, isn't it?"

"Yes, but it'll make us do something those girls will never do," Randi said. "Grow up."

Kate made a fist, and she and Randi bumped knuckles. "You go, girl."

"I think you mean *woman*," Randi said with a grin.

Kate chuckled and got out. She started to walk through the dark up the street toward her house. Despite the brief moment of levity she'd just shared with Randi, it was hard to remember a time in her life when she had felt as uncertain and insecure as she did right now. Maybe seventh grade, when being popular was all every girl strove for. But even then all of her insecurities had been focused on herself. This time it was a much broader sense of precariousness. Herself, her family, her friends. Danger and uncertainty lurked everywhere.

Kate walked up to the driveway gate. She was just about to key in the code to open it when a voice from the dark said, "Hold it!"

5

KATE FROZE IN THE DARK. POSSIBILITIES FLASHED through her head. Was it Stu and Tanner seeking revenge? The Blattarias?

"Put your hands on your head and turn around slowly," the voice ordered.

Kate did as she was told. As she turned, a flashlight burst on, blinding her. She started to lower her hands to shield her eyes.

"Keep those hands on your head!" the voice barked.

Kate kept her hands on her head and tried to squint through the light to see who it was, but the beam was too bright. She had to turn her head away slightly.

"Who are you?" the voice asked.

"Who are *you*?" Kate asked back, knowing that if he was part of any law enforcement agency, he was required by law to identify himself.

"Officer Dillon Connors, IAD," came the answer.

The Internal Affairs Department, Kate thought. The arm of

the police in charge of rooting out corruption within the force. "Can I see some ID?" she asked.

"I'm holding up my badge," he said.

"You're also holding a bright light to my face making it impossible to see," Kate said.

Officer Connors lowered the flashlight and aimed it at a wallet. Kate's eyes were still bleary from the bright light, but she thought she was looking at a photo ID and a silver badge. For the first time she got a sense of the person holding the wallet and flashlight. He was tall and broad shouldered, with neatly trimmed brown hair and a mustache.

"Now let's see some ID for you," Connors said, putting away the wallet.

"I don't have any." Since Randi had driven, all Kate had brought was lip gloss, cash, and a house key. "But I'm Kate Blessing, and this is where I live. Can I put my arms down? I feel really stupid standing here like this."

"Okay, but keep them in front of you where I can see them," Connors said.

Kate lowered her arms. Connors shined the flashlight beam in her face again.

"Can you please not do that?" Kate asked, shielding her eyes with her hand.

The IAD officer lowered the flashlight. "What are you doing out here?"

"I went for a walk."

"You always go for walks without ID in the dark?" Connors asked.

"Sometimes," Kate said. "What are *you* doing out here?"

Connors didn't answer. Maybe it wasn't necessary. Kate's father had been arrested for bribing members of the local police department. That was precisely the kind of thing the IAD had been created to investigate.

"All right, you can go," Connors said.

"That's it?" Kate asked, a bit ruefully. "No other questions?"

Again, Connors was silent. Kate keyed the code to open the gate and stepped in, then turned and watched it close, making sure Connors wasn't following. She knew he wasn't allowed to set foot on her property without a search warrant.

A moment later Kate let herself into the house. She was tired and worn out and eager to go to bed. She had a feeling it would be easy to fall asleep that night. In a strange way, knowing the cops were around made her feel safer.

Her cell phone rang. Kate opened her eyes. Her bedroom was filled with sunlight. Half asleep, Kate debated whether to answer or just let the phone ring. Whoever it was could wait. Unless . . .

Kate rolled over and reached down to the floor, pulling the phone out of her bag. As she squinted at the number she noticed the batteries were low. It was Teddy! In an instant she felt wide awake. "Hello?"

"Hey," Teddy said. "Did I wake you?"

"It's okay, I don't mind," Kate blurted as all the pent-up worries of the past few days flooded out of her. She was just so glad to hear his voice again.

"How are you?" He sounded cheerful, and Kate felt herself relax, as if she'd been tense in a hundred different places she wasn't even aware of. He sounded like he still liked her.

"I'm okay," she said. "It's good to hear your voice."

"Yours too," said Teddy.

Kate was tempted to ask why it had taken him so long to call, but she decided that might not be the best approach. Even though the past few days had been agony, she didn't want him to regret calling her.

"How's your dad?" Teddy asked.

"Not too good," Kate answered. "He's still in jail. How's your father?"

"He's . . ." Teddy hesitated as if unsure what to say. "He's calmed down."

"But still freaked out?" Kate guessed.

"Seriously, Blessing, can you blame him?" Teddy said. "It's got to be a shock to wake up one morning and read that your son's girlfriend's father has just been arrested for a slew of mob-related crimes."

Kate felt herself tensing again. The way he said it did make it sound pretty bad. "Then maybe the real question, Teddy, is how do *you* feel about it?"

"You know how I feel," Teddy said.

Kate thought she did. She *hoped* she did. But it was hard to be certain of anything at a time like this. The implications of her father's arrest seemed endless. Even now they were still materializing unexpectedly. Take, for instance, every young woman's fantasy: a beautiful wedding. Could she really imagine Teddy's parents—rich, socially connected, pillars of the community—agreeing to be photographed with her parents? And who would give away the bride if her father was still in prison?

But there was another, more urgent question pressing into her consciousness. Kate concentrated on sounding calm and asked in a nonchalant tone, "So, when will I see you again?"

The question was met with silence.

"Teddy?" Kate said.

"I . . ." There was a catch in his voice, and suddenly Kate felt a chill. "Blessing, listen, the truth is, my parents really are in turmoil over this. I think it's illogical, but right now they're not interested in what I think. I can't just ignore them or pretend they don't have a right to feel the way they do."

Kate felt herself tense even more. "Which means?"

"Sometimes you have to give a little to get a little," Teddy said.

Kate sensed that he was having trouble telling her what that little thing he had to give was. She took a deep breath, let it out slowly, and braced herself. "Okay, I'm ready."

"I'm sorry, Blessing, I really am," Teddy said. "The reason you haven't heard from me is because I've been fighting with them about this. I mean, it makes no sense—"

Oh, please, Teddy, Kate thought unhappily. *Enough with the buildup. Just tell me already.*

"I didn't call sooner because I wanted to wait until I was certain about what was going to happen," he said.

Something's going to happen, she thought. *And it's not going to be good.*

"Teddy, just tell me."

"They're sending me to the London office," Teddy said.

At first, Kate didn't understand. She heard the word "office" and thought of school. Teddy was being sent to the office? In London?

"The London office of my father's company," Teddy explained, as if he could feel her confusion through the telephone.

"But what about school?" she asked, still not completely comprehending

"What about it?" Teddy said.

"Don't you have to finish high school before you can go to work in your father's company?"

Teddy chuckled. "I really did wake you, didn't I? It's just for the summer, Blessing. Not even that, since it's already July and they want me back by the middle of August for the annual family holiday."

Kate took a moment to gather her thoughts. He was going away, but only for a little more than a month. That was bad news, but not terrible. Even if she factored in that family vacation, it wouldn't be long before he returned. And then senior year would start, and they'd be together again.

"When do you leave?" Kate asked.

There was another silence. And then Teddy said, "This afternoon."

What? This news hit Kate as hard as the news that he was leaving. "But when will I see you?" Kate asked. She knew she sounded desperate, and immediately chastised herself for it.

"Blessing, please try to understand—"

Kate was aware that Teddy was speaking, but his words weren't getting through. For the second time in her life she'd seriously given herself to someone who was going to vanish. Was it just really bad luck? Was it the men she chose? Or was there something wrong with her?

The phrase "only a month" caught her ear and brought her back.

"Sorry?" she said.

"I said don't forget, I'll only be gone a month," Teddy said.

Yes, yes, she'd already decided that a month was bad, but not horrible. She could wait a month. But somehow, if she could just see him for a moment before he left, she thought she would be able to deal with it.

"Teddy, I know this will sound silly," she said. "But is there any way I could see you before you go?"

"It doesn't sound silly at all," Teddy said. "I would have suggested it myself. I just don't know how."

"What if I come to the airport?" Kate asked.

"You'd do that?" Teddy sounded surprised.

"Of course," Kate said. She knew she must have sounded a little bit desperate. But after last weekend, how could he not understand how she felt?

"I'm flying British Airways, flight number forty-seven. It's scheduled to depart at seven. I plan to get to the airport no later than five."

"Promise you won't leave until I get there?" Kate said.

Teddy laughed. "I'll tell the pilot to hold the plane."

"You know what I mean," Kate said.

They spoke a little longer, and then Teddy said he had to get off. But that was okay. By then, Kate felt reassured. He still liked her. Going to London wasn't his idea, and it wasn't his fault. She might not like it, but she'd just have to deal.

She'd hardly closed the phone when it started to ring again. Kate recognized the number. It was Leo.

"Hey, what's up?" Kate answered.

"Sorry to bother you, Katie," Leo said. "But we got a problem."

6

"**B**ENNY'S WASTING NO TIME WORKING ON TAKING OVER the organization," Leo said.

Kate felt a chill. Her uncle Benny Hacksaw had been trying to take over her father's organization for years. Now that her father was behind bars, this was the perfect opportunity.

"What's he doing?" she asked.

"He took 'em all out fishing."

"Fishing?" Kate repeated. Somehow, this wasn't what she'd expected to hear. Nor did it sound particularly threatening.

"Hey, what do guys like to do?" Leo asked. "Get away from their wives and girlfriends, and drink. What better place to do it than on a boat?"

"Benny doesn't have a boat," Kate said.

"It's one of those chartered deals," Leo said. "This is the beginning, Katie. He'll start by wining and dining them. Then he'll suggest some scams. The next thing you know, they'll all be reporting to him."

Kate knew he was right. They had to do something to stop Benny, and the sooner they did it, the better. She'd said she was going to take over for her father, and now it was time to do it. She could feel a wave of nervousness and uncertainty wash over her. Was she really prepared to stand up to Uncle Benny? Did she have a choice?

"Any idea when they're coming back to the dock?" Kate asked.

"The charter boats?" Leo said. "They run like clockwork. Out every morning at eight, back at four."

Kate glanced at the time. She knew what she had to do. But did she have time to do it *and* see Teddy at the airport? She'd give it her best shot.

"I'll meet you at the dock at four," Kate said. .

"Right," Leo said.

Kate was just about to hang up when she thought of something else. "Leo, how many of our guys are on that boat?"

"I'm not sure, Kate. Anywhere from six to eight, is my guess."

"Thanks, see you there." Kate hung up. Before she got up, she slid open her desk drawer and reached in the back where she'd stashed the wads of money she'd found in the frozen broccoli package.

At the docks, Kate parked in the gravel lot and got out. The summer heat was intense, and the air was still and smelled like rotting fish. Seagulls watched her from their perches on the pilings. Half a dozen wooden docks stretched out into the bay. Even on this broiling hot day, most of the boats were docked.

Leo was sitting in his car with the engine running and the AC on. When he saw her, he got out of the car. Kate instantly noticed that he looked pale and drawn. His breathing seemed labored. Kate was immediately concerned. "Leo, are you okay?"

"Yeah, yeah," Leo said. "I'm fine. It's just this heat."

Kate pointed at the docks. "Know which boat they're on?"

"The *Snake Charmer*." Leo pointed at a large white sign that said SNAKE CHARMER. DAILY CHARTERS. SHARK. TUNA. STRIPERS. BLUES. Large, wrinkled, dried-out fish tails had been nailed to the sides of the sign.

"I wonder if Benny picked the boat just for the name," Kate mused.

A few boats were coming in, followed by squawking, diving seagulls. But each one passed the *Snake Charmer*'s dock. Katie checked her watch impatiently.

"Got someplace else to go?" Leo asked.

Kate nodded. "But this has to come first."

Leo took out a handkerchief and dabbed his forehead. His breathing still sounded rough and strained.

"Leo, why don't you wait in the car until they come, okay?" Kate said.

Without any argument, Leo got back into his car. Kate found some shade and stood in it. A short time later a large white boat turned down their row of docks. Kate spotted two of her father's crew, Joey Buttons and Sharktooth Ray, in the bow, drinking beers. She started to feel nervous. What if Uncle Benny got angry or challenged her?

The boat pulled up to the dock, and a crewman secured it with some ropes. The men began to climb up onto the dock. Almost all of them weaved and staggered. None noticed Kate standing at the end of the dock. Willy Shoes, another member of the organization, was the first one off.

"Welcome back, boys," Kate said, reaching into her bag and taking out a white envelope.

Willy Shoes looked up with surprise. "What is this, a home-coming party?"

"My father wants you to know how much he appreciates your loyalty," Kate said, handing him the envelope. She was aware that her hand was shaking, but Willy seemed too interested in what was inside the envelope to notice. He opened it and peeked inside. His eyes widened. He folded the envelope and slid it into his jacket.

"I hope that's enough to keep you going for a few weeks," Kate said.

"Are you kiddin'?" Willy said. "It's more than enough. Holy cow."

As each man came off the boat, Kate handed him an envelope. The men smelled of booze and fish—not a particularly appealing combination.

"Just remember, there's plenty more where that came from," Kate said.

"So how's your dad doing?" Sharktooth Ray asked as Kate handed him an envelope.

"He's doing fine," Kate said. "Danny thinks he's going to get out any day now."

"You sure?" Antoine asked. "We heard he got slapped with a huge bail."

"Who told you that?" Kate asked, reaching into her bag for the next envelope.

"The newspaper, sweetheart." It was her uncle Benny, holding his hand out for an envelope like all the others.

Kate felt her heart begin to thud. She hesitated before giving him the envelope. "Don't believe everything you read."

Benny waited with his hand out. "Hey, don't I get an envelope too? Ain't I the second in command?"

"You know what this is for, Benny?" Kate said, holding back the envelope.

"Sure. Sonny's takin' care of us," Benny said. "It's what a good boss does. And it's why his crew stays loyal to him while he's away."

Kate reluctantly handed him an envelope. Then she turned to the group. "Now listen up, guys. My dad has a message for you. Nothing changes while he's away. I know the factory got hit bad"—Kate gave Uncle Benny a look—"but as long as the other operations keep going, we should be okay. Especially when I've got these nice white envelopes to hand out."

The factory—where knockoff clothes and accessories and DVDs were produced—had been the Blessing organization's cash cow until someone ransacked it. Uncle Benny insisted it was the Blattarias' doing, but Kate wasn't so sure.

"What if we got questions or need to talk to him about stuff?" Joey Buttons asked.

"I don't think going to see him is such a good idea," Kate said. "I mean, not unless you want the feds to know who you are. But they already know who I am and I go to see him every week, so just let me know what you want and I'll make sure he gets the message."

"Sounds pretty good," said Willy.

"I'll say." Sharktooth Ray patted his pocket. "As long as these envelopes keep coming, what's to complain about?"

The men went off to their cars. Benny had gotten into his big black Mercedes and rolled slowly toward her. He stopped and brought down the window. The AC was on, and a cloud of cold cigar smoke wafted out as he squinted up at her.

"Nice move," he said in a sourly begrudging tone. "You're good, know that?"

"I learned from the best," Kate replied.

"Too bad you and I both know the best ain't good enough," Benny snarled. "At least, not as long as the feds got your father. And my information tells me that this is one case when you *can* believe what you read. He ain't goin' anywhere for a long, long time."

Kate shrugged dismissively. "I wouldn't be so sure, Benny."

Her uncle smiled. He picked up his white envelope and tapped it against the steering wheel. "The envelopes are a nice touch. But here's what I want to know. What happens when the money in them runs out?"

"Who said they're going to run out?" Kate asked.

Benny smirked. "That old freezer ain't that big, Kate. And

don't be surprised if one of these days you open one of those packages and instead of wads of hundreds, you find green beans."

The window went back up, and the Mercedes rolled away, leaving Kate shaken. Perhaps she should have known that Benny, being the second in command, would know about her father's secret stash of cash. But it rattled her just the same.

She walked over to Leo's car and got in. The cold air of the AC was a welcome respite from the summer heat.

"How'd it go?" Leo asked.

Kate shrugged. "Just okay. I think the guys bought it, but not Benny."

"He took the two thousand like everyone else," Leo said.

"Why not?" said Kate. "Who would turn down free money?"

"Well, at least you bought yourself some time," Leo said.

"I know," Katie agreed. "I just don't know how much time."

Speaking of time, Kate thought, and checked the dashboard clock. It was 4:27!

"Gotta scoot." Kate leaned over and gave Leo a kiss on the cheek, then hopped out of his car and dashed over to hers. A moment later she'd raced out of the marina parking lot and down some back roads to the highway.

But it was rush hour, and the highway traffic was crawling. Kate found herself stuck behind a big semi tractor trailer with cars on both sides. She felt like banging her hands against the steering wheel and screaming that this was completely unfair!

Kate kept one eye on the back of the tractor trailer and the other on the clock. Teddy said he'd be at the airport at five p.m.

He'd have to check in and then go through security. And after that, she'd have no chance to see him.

Finally, she could see the tall, thin airport control tower in the distance off to her right. The clock said 5:17. If she could just get there in the next few minutes, she still might have a chance. . . .

Just then the traffic stopped altogether. Kate had no idea why. All she could see in front of her was the truck. She was jammed in on both sides by bumper-to-bumper traffic. If not, she might have steered off the highway and tried the shoulder.

5:18 . . . 5:19 . . .

She took out her phone and called him, but got his voice mail. "Teddy, if you get this before you take off, I'm stuck in traffic. Call me, okay?"

5:21 . . . 5:22 . . .

Traffic wasn't moving. With each passing minute, Kate felt the hope drain out of her.

5:23 . . . 5:24 . . .

She tried his cell again and got voice mail again. By now he would have checked in and gotten into the line to go through security.

5:27 . . . 5:28 . . .

She could see the entrance to the airport up ahead. Part of her was asking, *What's the use? By now he's past security.* But another part said, *Don't give up. You never know. There could be a delay.*

5:37 . . .

She turned into the airport entrance and headed for the international departures terminal. There she parked in short-term parking and hurried into the terminal. As she'd expected, there was no sign of Teddy on the check-in line. She hurried toward security. On the way she passed the monitors. BA Flt 47 was scheduled for an on-time takeoff. Kate rushed toward the security area. A long line of people were waiting to go through the metal detectors. Kate searched in vain for Teddy's blond head, but there was no sign of him.

She tried his phone yet again: voice mail. Kate hung her head. Instead of leaving, she walked back toward the check-in, just on the slim chance that Teddy had been late. But it was now close to 5:56. Teddy's plane would be boarding in half an hour and leaving in an hour.

Kate walked back out to the parking area and got her car. She thought she'd leave the airport and go home, but what was the rush? There'd be no one there waiting for her. On second thought, she drove around to the road beside the runways. Maybe she would get to see Teddy, or at least his plane.

She parked . . . and started to cry.

7

SHE WAS DRYING HER TEARS WHEN HER PHONE RANG. *Teddy!?* She eagerly grabbed the phone and checked the number. It was Randi. At first she didn't think she would answer. But what good would wallowing in this depression do? Talking to her best friend might help.

"Hello?"

"You won't believe what those—" Randi began, but then caught herself. "Whoa, what's wrong?"

"Nothing," Kate said.

"Yeah, right," Randi scoffed. "Come on, share."

"Teddy's going to London for the rest of the summer," Kate said with a sniff.

"That wasn't in the plans," Randi said.

Kate explained that it had been Teddy's parents' decision.

"At least you'll get to see him in the fall," Randi said.

"Right."

"So where are you now?"

"At the airport," Kate said.

"Huh?"

Kate told her how she'd tried to get there in time to say good-bye but had arrived too late.

"So . . . why are you still there?" Randi asked.

"Because . . . I know he's not far away." Kate felt the tears come back. She started to sob softly.

"Aw, Kate, I'm so sorry," Randi sympathized.

Kate got her tears under control. "So you were saying I wouldn't believe something?"

"Those bastards Stu and Tanner," Randi said. "They keyed my car last night. We didn't see it in the dark, but this morning I found it. On both sides. Totally ruined the paint job."

"That's awful," Kate said.

"Those guys suck," Randi growled.

"But maybe it's good, in a way," Kate said.

"How's that?" Randi asked uncertainly.

"Maybe they'll feel like they got even now and they'll leave you alone," Kate said.

"They'd *better* feel like they've gotten even," Randi said. "Because they've gotten way more than even. It's going to cost me a ton to get it fixed."

"Well, I guess we're lucky our little venture is paying off," Kate said.

"I guess," Randi said with a sigh. "Anyway, want to do something tonight?"

"I don't know," Kate said. "Can I let you know later?"

"Sure," Randi said. "Just don't sit home alone and mope all night, okay? It's so much more fun when we mope together."

Kate chuckled. No matter how down she was, Randi always seemed to be able to get a small laugh out of her. "I'll call you later, okay?"

"Sure."

Kate closed the phone and watched the planes land and take off. Just after seven p.m. a British Airways 747 lifted off the runway. The red and blue stripes of the Union Jack were painted on the tail. Sunlight glanced off the plane's long, white body. Kate sat in her car and once again felt tears run down her cheeks. If only she'd been able to say good-bye and wish him a safe trip. If only he'd held her in his arms and kissed and hugged her and promised that the month would go quickly and everything would be fine.

It was close to eight o'clock when Kate got home. The sun was low in the west, sending long shadows across the roads. A white van with the words DOMINIC'S POOL SERVICE on the side was parked outside the driveway gate. This had to be some kind of mistake, Kate thought as she drove up behind it. They didn't use a pool service. Her father had always insisted on taking care of the pool himself. Kate always suspected that there was something thera-peutic about it that relaxed him.

Kate pulled her car up behind the van and got out. In the van's side-view mirror, Kate could see a guy with sunglasses sitting in the front seat watching her. She walked up to the window.

"I think there's some kind of mistake," she said.

"I don't think so."

Kate recognized the voice and blinked with astonishment. "Nick?"

"I think you mean Dominic," Nick said with a funny accent. "Here to take care of your pool. What do you say you open the gate and let me in, okay?"

Kate was wary. What did he want? She tried to glance into the back of the truck.

"It's just me," Nick said, lowering his voice. "No tricks."

"What do you want?" Kate asked.

"Hey, I'm just trying to help you out here, lady," Nick said, still pretending to speak like some sort of New Yorker or something. "The boss says he owes you a favor."

It was true that Nick owed her a favor. After the factory was ransacked, she'd warned him that Uncle Benny was trying to lay the blame on the Blattarias. But Kate still didn't know what to do. With her father in jail, this was the perfect time for the Blattarias to move in and take over once and for all. Meanwhile, the charade must have been for the benefit of any FBI guys hiding in the woods with shotgun microphones that could pick up conversations from a long way off.

"Look, I ain't got all day," Nick continued with the charade. "Like I said, I'm just trying to do you a favor. You ain't interested, I'll go." He leaned closer and whispered, "For Christ's sake, I'm risking my neck to be here, Kate."

He sounded sincere. Kate decided it was worth the risk. She

went over to the key pad and opened the gate so that Nick could drive the van in. She followed in her car. At the house, Nick got out of the truck wearing white coveralls. It had been weeks since she'd been this close to him, and her memory of those magnetic blue eyes and handsome face with that cleft chin had dimmed somewhat. He was indeed handsome, but his looks did nothing for her at the moment. Right now, she was seriously missing Teddy.

He went around to the back of the truck and took out a white plastic bucket with some chemicals in it. Kate knew better than to question what he was doing. Instead, she walked with him around to the back of the house. Nick paused by the pool and looked around.

"Something I can help you with?" Kate asked.

"Where's your pool filter?" Nick asked.

This made no sense. They both knew Nick wasn't there to clean her pool.

"Nick, what's going on?" Kate asked.

Nick gave her a frustrated look. "Listen, lady, I'm Dominic. I don't know who Nick is. But if you don't show me that filter soon, I'm out of here."

Kate decided to play along, partly out of curiosity and partly because he was already there, so what did it matter? "It's back here," she said, leading him to a small pool house. Inside, the pool house smelled of chlorine and the filter hummed. Kate waited while Nick put his hands on his hips and studied the filter. He reached down and adjusted a knob, and the pool house filled with a gurgling noise not unlike a washing machine.

"That should do it," Nick said in a low voice, just barely audible over the sound of the filter.

"What'd you do?" Kate asked.

"I increased the amount of air running through the system," Nick said. "It won't hurt anything." He looked around. "But it should make it noisy enough so that we can't be heard by any hidden mikes."

"My dad had this place swept thoroughly just a few weeks ago," Kate said.

"By Dee Bug?" Nick grinned.

Kate's stomach dropped. Obviously Nick knew something she didn't know. "They were FBI?" she asked.

Nick shook his head. "Our guys."

"Your guys?" Kate said. "That makes no sense. Why are we talking so quietly if they're your guys? Why do you care if they hear us?"

Nick pressed a finger to his lips. "Because I'm not here, okay?"

Kate didn't understand what game he was playing. But whatever it was, she wasn't interested. "What's going on? I mean it, Nick. Either you tell me right now or you can go."

"How are you?" Nick asked.

Kate rolled her eyes is disbelief. "I'm fine, thanks. How are you and Tiff?"

Nick's shoulders sagged. "Why do you always have to bring her up?"

"Oh, let's see." Kate pressed her finger against her lips and gazed upward as if deep in thought. "I know! Maybe because you lied about not seeing her? Maybe because you were seeing her when you seduced me? Maybe because you were still seeing her when you pretended you were only seeing me?"

Nick stared at the floor and ran his fingers though his dark hair.

Kate found herself wishing he'd at least try to deny it. "Well?"

He raised his hands helplessly. "Look, that's what guys do."

Kate stared at him in disbelief as months' worth of repressed anger boiled up inside her. "*That's* your best explanation? It's what guys do? Well, let me tell you something, Mr. Casanova. That may be what guys do, but it's not what guys do *to me*. Understand? Now I've had enough of this crap. Either tell me why you're here, or get out."

"Okay, just try to keep it down, will you?" Nick said. "I came here to tell you I didn't know anything about the factory hit."

"Oh, give me a break," Kate said. "I am so tired of your lies." She turned to leave the pool house, but Nick held her arm and tried to stop her. She angrily shook out of his grip. "Don't you ever touch me again. Do you understand?"

Nick grit his teeth. "Just listen. I didn't say we didn't do it. I said I didn't know about it."

Once again, Kate was confused. "Why tell me?"

"Because I want you to know, okay?" Nick said.

"Why? Why do you care?" Kate asked. "I don't get this, Nick. I really don't. You cheated on me. You lied to me. And now what is this? Can you give me the slightest reason why I should believe a word you say?"

Nick's face darkened. Kate had never seen him blush before. It was almost as if she were watching water come to a boil. "You know, you are just . . . !" he started to blurt, then caught himself.

"Just what?" Kate demanded. "Don't hold back, Nick. Or is it just so ingrained in your nature not to show your real feelings?"

"You . . . you . . ." Suddenly, he stepped close, enveloped her in his arms, and pressed his lips against hers. Kate's mind went blank, and her body was awash with emotion. This was wrong! So wrong! She was supposed to be kissing Teddy, not Nick! But something unexpected took hold of her. Something she'd thought she'd managed to get out of her system. But here it was, as strong as ever. She held him tight and kissed back with unexpected passion.

Was she out of her mind? After everything he'd done to her!?

Suddenly Kate pushed him away. Nick scowled at her as if he didn't understand why.

"Why did you do that?" she asked. "What's wrong with you? Isn't Tiff enough? Haven't you already done enough to me?"

"Tiff isn't in the picture anymore," Nick said.

"Oh, right," Kate scoffed. "Like I haven't heard that one before."

"It's true," Nick said.

Kate gazed at him suspiciously. "It didn't look that way two weeks ago, when you were kissing her passionately outside Club Che in Bronson Park."

"I'm telling you, it's over," Nick insisted.

"You've told me that before," Kate said. "Come on, Nick, can't you at least come up with something new?"

Nick let out a long, frustrated sigh. Something about his reaction made Kate feel inclined to believe him. But was she seeing this clearly? With Teddy gone and her father in jail, was she so desperate for something to hang on to that she wanted to believe him despite common sense? *Get a grip, Kate!* she told herself.

"Okay, suppose it *is* over between you and Tiff," Kate said. "Congratulations. So what am I? The next best thing?"

"Did it ever occur to you that maybe *you're* the reason that Tiff isn't in the picture?" Nick asked.

Kate blinked uncertainly. Actually, *that* had not occurred to her. But she still wasn't sure. It was such an easy line to toss out there. And just what every girl wanted to hear. "Why now and not six months ago?" she asked.

Nick hung his head and stared at the pool house floor. He scuffed his shoe against some loose grains of blue chemical that lay there. Finally, he looked back up at her. "I don't know. You want the truth? That's the truth, okay? Maybe sometimes the answer is, there is no answer." He tapped a finger against his head. "If it were up to this, I'd say no way. We're enemies. This'll never work. It's craziness. But it's not up to this. For six months I haven't been able to get you out of my mind. I wake up in the morning and I think about you. I drive to Atlantic City and I think about you. I fly to Las Vegas and I think about you. What am I supposed to do?"

Take me in your arms and kiss me again, Kate thought, surprising herself.

But he couldn't read her mind and didn't know that's what she was thinking. Maybe it was for the best. She still wasn't ready to forgive him. Not yet, and maybe never. *Fool me once, shame on you. Fool me twice, shame on me.*

"Here's what you can do," Kate said. "You can prove it. Talk is cheap. You can't tell me anything I haven't heard before."

Nick raised an eyebrow. "Oh, yeah? You want me to prove it? How about this? My father ordered the hit on your factory, but he didn't tell me, okay? For whatever reason, he didn't want me to know. That's the truth."

"It's just words to me," Kate said. "It doesn't mean anything."

"Okay, here's something that will mean something," Nick said with a smile. "Tonight around one a.m. a semi tractor trailer filled with all the goods we stole from you is gonna be parked in the lot behind the Turnpike Diner. The driver's gonna be inside eating dinner. Rumor has it he keeps a spare key under the passenger-side floor mat."

Kate was flabbergasted. "You're giving back all the stuff you took? Why?"

Nick smiled. "Because, like you said, talk is cheap." He leaned close and kissed her on the cheek. Then he picked up the white plastic bucket and left.

8

T COULD HAVE BEEN A TRAP, BUT KATE DIDN'T THINK SO.
What did the Blattarias have to gain? Nothing, as far as Kate
could see. But maybe she wasn't seeing all of it. Maybe there
was more. If only she could talk to her father about it. No, wait!
This was exactly the sort of situation her father used to speak to
her mother about. So why couldn't she do the same?

It was almost eight thirty now. Kate got into her car and drove
to her mother's apartment at the River House. She buzzed the
apartment.

"Yeah?" Her brother, Sonny Jr., answered.

"It's Kate."

The door buzzed, and Kate went in and took the elevator up.
Her brother met her at the door. Kate stopped and stared at him
in surprise. She'd just seen him a week ago, but he looked different. "Have you gotten taller?"

Sonny Jr. grinned with pleasure. "A little, but Mom says it's
also because I've been caddying a lot and all that exercise has

helped me slim down. You know how being thinner helps you look taller?"

"That's great," Kate said. "So, is Mom here?"

"She's supposed to be, but she's late," Sonny Jr. said. "You want to stick around? She should be home pretty soon."

"Okay," Kate said, realizing she hadn't eaten since lunch. "Anything to eat?"

"You kidding?" Sonny Jr. asked. "This is Mom's place. There's *always* stuff to eat."

Kate went into the kitchen and found a bowl of fruit on the counter and yogurt in the fridge. Instead of going back to the TV or whatever he'd been doing, Sonny Jr. picked out a peach and joined her. Kate couldn't understand what had gotten into her brother, who usually acted like he didn't want to be anywhere near her.

"Have you seen Dad yet?" Kate asked him.

Sonny Jr. nodded pensively. "Yeah. Mom drove me over."

Kate felt an unexpected glimmer of hope. "Did she see him too?"

Her brother shook his head. "Didn't want to. Sucks, huh?"

"Totally." The glimmer went out. Kate wasn't sure how much her brother knew about the options that lay before them—either going "fatherless" for a long time to come, or changing their identities and moving far away from Riverton forever.

"How's Teddy?" Sonny Jr. asked. "I haven't seen him around the club lately."

Teddy had gotten Sonny Jr. the caddying job at his country club, Eagle Crest.

"He's . . ." Kate hesitated, feeling horribly guilty. Teddy was somewhere in the air over the Atlantic and she'd already found herself in Nick's arms. This was so not the way it was supposed to be. "He's gone to London for a month."

Sonny Jr. frowned. It wasn't that he felt bad for Kate, although perhaps he did. But he'd also come to like Teddy.

"What's new around here?" Kate asked.

Sonny Jr.'s forehead wrinkled, and he leaned toward her. In a whisper, he said, "I don't think things are going so good between Mom and Marvin."

Kate couldn't quite understand why her brother had dropped her voice, since their mother wasn't even in the apartment. But that wasn't important. The news was. "How do you know?" she asked.

"I hear things," Sonny Jr. said. "Like when she's on the phone with him."

"Like what?"

"I think he wants to get married, and he doesn't understand why she doesn't want to."

"Maybe because she's still married to Dad," Kate said with a wink.

"Yeah, well, I guess Marvin wants her to get divorced and she doesn't want to," Sonny Jr. said.

"Does she say why not?" Kate asked.

"Sort of," Sonny Jr. said. "Mostly she says she isn't ready and she doesn't know and it's too soon and stuff like that."

To Kate, this sounded like good news. Was it possible that her mother was not ready to give up on her father?

The front door opened and closed and a moment later Amanda entered the kitchen. At first she appeared troubled by something, but when she saw Kate she brightened. "Well, well, to what do I owe this surprise visit?"

Kate quickly shot her eyes at Sonny Jr. so her mother would know that she needed to speak to her in private. They went into the bedroom and sat on the bed. Kate told her mother about the truck.

"How do you know about this?" Amanda asked.

"I . . . Nick Blattaria told me," Kate answered reluctantly.

Kate's mother could not have been more surprised if Kate had announced that she'd decided to become a nun. Amanda stared at her daughter with eyes widened by disbelief. "You were never supposed to talk to him again."

"Something came up," Kate said. "Purely business." And before Amanda could inquire further, Kate quickly went on to tell her the plan she had for hijacking the truck.

"What do you think?" she asked when she'd finished.

"It sounds very well thought out," her mother said, once again giving her daughter a quizzical look.

"What is it, Mom?" Kate asked.

"I'm just . . . impressed," Amanda said.

Kate beamed proudly.

Kate spent the rest of the day organizing and briefing the crew. No one questioned her authority for an instant. That night the truck hijacking went off without incident. Antoine and

Sharktooth Ray drove the semi to a warehouse in South End where Kate had arranged for a buyer to wait for them. Kate, Willy Shoes, Joey Buttons, and Leo followed in Willy's car. The buyer went through the goods in the back of the truck and then he and Kate haggled over the price.

A few hours later, with daylight just beginning to break, the crew sat around her breakfast table eating eggs and bacon and dividing the take. When they finished, each man walked away with enough cash to keep going for the next couple of months.

Finally, it was just Kate and Leo and a bunch of dirty dishes and pans. Even though the sun was rising and Kate had not yet slept, she started to load the dishwasher.

"Leave it, Kate," Leo said with a yawn.

"I can't," Kate answered. "It's not my style."

Leo started to roll up his sleeves. "Then we'll do it together and get it done fast." He brought a bunch of dirty dishes over to the sink. "So, how does it feel?"

Kate knew what he meant. "Feels good, Leo. The whole thing went off as planned. We made some good money. What else is there?"

"You got the guys' respect," Leo said. "They listened and did exactly what you told them to do. Your father would be proud. I'm proud of you."

"Thanks, Leo," Kate said. She could do it. She could lead the Blessing organization if she had to.

9

THE MONTH TEDDY SPENT IN LONDON WENT SLOWLY, but at least Kate was able to IM him in the morning when it was afternoon over there and, when it was afternoon here, she spoke with him via Skype in the apartment where he was living because it was night in London. He always sounded eager to speak to her and talked often about how much he missed her. Together they counted the days until his return.

But Kate's hopes of seeing him between London and the annual Fitzgerald family summer vacation were dashed when Teddy's parents suddenly decided that they wanted to spend their annual summer vacation at a private villa on the island of Ibiza off the southern coast of Spain. And that it would be best if Teddy flew directly from London to Spain without coming home first.

"Have they ever done that before?" Kate asked on her computer microphone as disappointment welled up in her.

"No," Teddy answered from his computer. "They've always taken the August vacation at the house on Twelve Mile Island."

"So they're breaking with tradition," Kate said.

"Blessing, I don't know what to say except I'm sorry," Teddy said. "Seriously, I'm amazed at the lengths they're going to to keep us from seeing each other. I just don't get it."

"Why not ask them?" Kate asked.

"I did, and they pretended it had nothing to do with you and me. They insist it's just time to do something different. Not that I believe them for an instant."

"You really think they're doing all this just to keep us apart?" Kate asked. "Doesn't it seem a little extreme?"

"I can only guess that they know how deeply I feel about you," Teddy said.

The news should have been music to Kate's ears, but it saddened her. If his parents were willing to go to these lengths—sending him to London for the summer, breaking tradition and going to Spain, sending him to boarding school—how could she and Teddy possibly fight them?

"Listen, I know this is disappointing, but don't let it get you down," Teddy said. "As long as we feel the way we feel about each other, there's nothing my parents can do to change it. They can try, but eventually we're going to see each other no matter what, right?"

"Right," Kate said, although she wasn't really sure she believed it.

"We'll just have to wait a little longer," Teddy said.

"So when will I see you?" Kate asked.

"After the vacation, I guess," Teddy said. "There's no way

my parents can keep me from coming home before I go off to school."

Kate hung up feeling depressed. She believed Teddy when he said that in the long run his parents couldn't keep them apart, but how long would the long run be? How long would she have to wait? Sometimes it seemed like everyone around her was living life while she was going to school, taking care of family business, and waiting for Teddy.

"I'm picking you up around noon tomorrow," Randi said after Kate told her that she'd now have to wait an additional two weeks before seeing Teddy again.

"Why?" Kate asked.

"Because that's what friends are for, right?"

The next day Randi arrived as promised. When Kate stepped out of the house she noticed that the sky was clear blue and the air comfortably warm and dry. In other words, it was perfect outside.

"Hop in," Randi said after turning down the car radio.

Kate got into the Lexus, and Randi turned up the music and started to drive.

"Where are we going?" Kate asked.

"The boat show," Randi said.

"Why?" Kate asked.

"Two reasons," Randi said. "First, because it's a beautiful day to be outdoors and it's an outdoor boat show. And two, because I have no idea what else to do."

"I don't know about you, but I was happy to stay home," Kate said.

"I think you mean you're happy to stay home and be unhappy," Randi corrected her. "Sorry, but today's about putting the word 'fun' back into Little Miss Have No Fun."

"And what about tomorrow?" Kate asked.

Randi glanced at her with a critical look. "Are you aware of how pathetic that sounds? It's like, 'Oh, dear, you may have saved me from myself today, but promise I'll be allowed to be miserable tomorrow.'"

Kate couldn't help smiling slightly. It did sound a little pathetic.

"Bull's-eye!" Randi said.

The boat show was in the parking lot at the fairgrounds, and Kate had to admit that she was surprised to see how crowded it was. The parking area was packed with cars, and had there been walls around the boats, it would have been wall-to-wall people. Randi paid their admission, and she and Kate joined the throngs wandering around among the tall white hulls of cabin cruisers and speedboats.

"What do we do?" Kate asked.

Randi pointed at a line of people waiting to climb carpeted stairs up to a large yacht. "We look in boats. Let's go look in that one."

They waited on line and then took a tour. Kate had to admit that she was surprised and impressed by how comfortable and well-decorated they were. Especially the galleys, which had every possible kitchen appliance.

But by the third boat, it was starting to get repetitive. Even

Randi had to admit that it was a little boring. "Are we having fun yet? Sorry, rhetorical question. Don't answer it."

Then Kate noticed something curious. Off to one side of the show was a large, aboveground swimming pool. About a dozen people all wearing tight black T-shirts were standing in it. Many of them were wearing swimming masks and snorkels.

"Come on," Kate said, tugging Randi by the sleeve. "Let's take a look."

"At a swimming pool?" Randi said. "What's so interesting about that?"

"Not the pool," Kate said. "What they're *doing* in the pool."

Randi scowled. "They're diving."

Kate looked again. She was right. The tight black T-shirts were actually short-sleeve wet suits, and the people in the pool were wearing tanks.

"Let's go," Kate said.

"Why?" asked Randi.

"I want to try it," Kate said.

"How do you know you can try it?" Randi asked.

"Why else would all those people be in that pool?" Kate asked.

It was clear from the way Randi had slowed down that she wasn't interested. "If you only knew how long it took me to do my hair this morning."

"So then I'll do it," Kate said. "I've always wanted to try scuba. There's no line right now."

"What about a bathing suit?" Randi asked.

"Wet suit," said Kate.

Randi gave her a sour look.

"I thought the whole idea of today was to put the fun back into Little Miss No Fun's life," Kate said.

"Be my guest," Randi said.

With Randi holding her bag, Kate went into a changing tent and put on a wet suit. It was a "shorty suit" with short sleeves and legs. On a platform next to the pool, a man wearing a wet suit with a PADI logo helped her put on the equipment. The pool was filled only to waist deep and was full of beginning divers of all shapes and sizes.

"Just breathe normally," the instructor advised. "And watch where you're going."

The gear was heavy, and he helped her into the pool. The truth was, Kate had always wanted to try scuba diving but had always been afraid of sinking to the bottom and not being able to swim back up. So trying it first in waist-deep water was perfect.

Even with the gear, the first breath underwater was hard to take, but once she did, the rest came surprisingly easy. The next thing she knew, she was swimming through a forest of human legs and other first-time scuba divers. There were so many people in the pool that she had to be careful not to run into anyone or be hit by a flapping black fin.

Several of the divers were playing with large, bullet-shaped devices with small propellers in them. By holding on to handles, the divers were pulled around the pool without having to kick. The divers using them must have thought they were fun, but Kate felt like they were annoying, if not dangerous. After one guy nearly hit her twice, Kate stopped swimming and stood up in the middle of the pool. The next time the guy passed, she tapped him on the head.

The guy stopped and stood up, pulling his mask off. He was slightly shorter than Kate but was solidly built, with broad shoulders. He appeared to be good-looking, but it was hard to tell thanks to the red outline of the mask on his face.

"You want something?" he asked.

"Yeah," Kate said. "I want you to be more careful. You almost hit me twice with that thing."

The guy frowned. "Maybe *you* should watch where *you're* going."

In that instant Kate realized she was looking for a fight. Not surprising, considering how frustrated and unhappy she'd been lately.

"That's the stupidest thing I've ever heard," she snapped. "It's like driving your car into a crowd of pedestrians and saying it was their fault for not getting out of the way."

The guy blinked with astonishment. "What's your problem?"

"My problem is that the world is filled with morons like you," Kate snapped.

Someone started to laugh. Kate turned. Nick, with a diving mask pushed up on his plastered-down black hair, was standing next to them. With a jolt, Kate realized that he'd been the other guy bombing around the pool with a propeller device.

"What?—" Kate began to ask what he was doing there, but the answer was obvious. He was doing the same thing she was.

"I thought being in water is supposed to relax people," Nick said.

"You know this chick?" asked the stocky guy.

"Kate, meet Tuna," Nick said, and turned to the stocky guy. "It's cool, Kate and I go way back."

"Oh, yeah?" Tuna said. "Well, she's definitely got some problems."

Kate snorted derisively. "I wouldn't talk."

"Tuna, go jump in a lake," Nick said with a grin. "Check that. Jump in a pool."

Tuna slipped his mask back on and flapped his flippers away.

"Fun, huh?" Nick said.

"It would be more fun if you boys didn't always feel the need to play with toys," Kate said.

"You sound kind of stressed," Nick said. "Things not going well?"

"Things are going fine," Kate replied.

"That's not what I hear," Nick said. "I hear there's a serious power struggle taking place now that your dad's not around."

Kate had no intention of discussing it with him. She pulled her mask on, swam back to the platform, and climbed out. Her scuba diving was over for the day.

Randi was waiting for her outside the changing tent. Kate's combed wet hair hung straight down to her shoulders.

"Have fun?" Randi asked.

Kate decided not to mention Nick. "Uh-huh. You should have tried it."

"Was I imagining things or did you stop to talk to two guys?" Randi asked.

"They were just a couple of jerks making it hard for everyone else to swim," Kate said.

Randi gave her an uncertain look. "You sure? It sort of looked like you knew one of them."

"No way." Kate shook her head. Now she noticed that Randi was gazing past her. Kate turned just as Nick and Tuna approached.

"So what are you doing here, anyway?" Nick asked her. "Shopping for a yacht?"

"Actually, just leaving," Kate replied.

"We are?" Randi sounded surprised.

"Want to introduce me to your friend?" Nick asked innocently.

Kate smiled, but behind her lips, her jaw was clenched tight. "Randi, this is Nick Blattaria, and his friend Tuna."

Randi looked confused. "I thought you said you didn't—"

"You must have misunderstood," Kate cut her short. "Nick's an old family friend." She pretended to check her watch. "Gosh, look at the time. We'd better leave or we'll be late for you know what."

"We do?" Randi looked completely baffled. Kate wished she'd just play along.

"Anyone hungry?" Nick asked. "How about I treat everyone to some sausages and beer?"

"I could go for that," Randi said. Now Kate noticed that her friend and Tuna were exchanging looks. *Perfect!* she thought miserably. *A double date with the enemy!*

"Could you excuse us for a second?" Kate asked, and pulled Randi out of earshot.

"What's going on?" Randi whispered.

"We are not eating lunch with those two," Kate whispered.

"Why not?"

"Because his father is my father's enemy," Kate said.

"But he seems nice and he's hot," Randi said.

"It looked to me like you were more interested in Tuna," Kate said.

"I am," Randi said. "I was thinking about Nick for you."

If only you knew, Kate thought. Randi knew nothing of her past relationship with Nick. Kate had kept it a secret. "I don't think so," Kate said.

"Oh, come on." Randi slid her arm through Kate's and started to walk her back toward the boys. "What's the big deal? Teddy's off in London, and then he's going to Ibiza. Believe me, he's not going to spend his days sitting inside missing you. It can't hurt to have lunch."

There was a lot of truth to that. And it would be better than sitting in her house alone. What harm could lunch do?

Nick treated everyone to lunch, and they sat at a picnic table. Nick was charming and funny and in no time he had Randi under his spell. Even Tuna, whose real name was Charlie, was a funny guy.

"So how'd you get your nickname?" Randi asked.

"You know those ads for Star-Kist tuna?" Tuna said. "They have this talking tuna named Charlie the Tuna. When I was a little kid, I just loved him. I don't know why. Maybe because we were both named Charlie."

"So people started calling you Tuna?" Randi said.

"Yeah."

"Do you even like tuna?" Kate couldn't help asking.

Tuna shrugged and smiled slyly. "Not really."

They laughed. As much as Kate didn't want to admit it, she was having fun. They finished eating, and then Randi and Tuna decided they wanted to get ice cream and went off before Kate could suggest that she and Randi should leave. By then it was clear to Kate that Randi was interested in Tuna (was there a guy she *wasn't* interested in?) and Kate doubted she would have been able to drag Randi away regardless. It was even possible that Nick had mentioned to Tuna in advance that he wanted to be alone with her.

Now Nick smiled across the picnic table at her. "Beautiful day, huh?"

"I don't know what you think you're doing, Nick," Kate said. "But whatever it is, it's not going to work."

10

ICK RAISED HIS HANDS AND PRETENDED TO BE
surprised. "Hey, all I did was invite you to have a beer
and an Italian sausage."

Kate rolled her eyes to let him know he wasn't fooling her. "Listen, Nick, it may be a coincidence that we ran into each other here. But don't bother trying to convince me that you don't have an agenda, because we both know you do. So here's what you need to know." Kate counted on her fingers. "One, my boyfriend is coming home from vacation soon, and I can't wait to see him. Two, everyone knows my uncle Benny wants to take over the Blessing organization, but it's not going to happen because everyone also knows that he's a hothead and an idiot. And three, everybody knows your father wants to take over our territory, but that's not going to happen either because my dad's crew is going to stay loyal to him no matter what. And that's that."

"Not really," Nick said, and then held up his own fingers and counted. "Now here's the way I see it. One, I don't know who this boyfriend is, but I do know that you couldn't have been thinking much about him a few days ago when we were in your pool house. Two, your uncle Benny may be a hothead and an idiot, but he's a cagey idiot and if you were smart you wouldn't be so quick to underestimate him. And three, as far as taking over your territory is concerned, it's not a matter of if. It's a matter of when. You and I both know we've already started, and if you had any sense, you'd accept it and figure out how to profit from it instead of trying to fight it."

"Well, I guess we see it differently, don't we?" Kate said, getting up. "Thanks for the sausage, Nick."

Nick also rose. "Kate, wait." His voice was laced with frustration.

Kate stopped, but shook her head. "No. No more words, Nick. I've told you before, I can't believe what you say anymore."

"Then what am I supposed to do?" Nick asked.

Kate locked eyes with him. "I don't know, Nick. And the reason I don't know is I've never been in a situation where I've had to try to believe someone who's lied repeatedly to me."

Nick pursed his lips in frustration.

"Looks like you've dug yourself a pretty deep hole," Kate said. She walked over to the ice-cream stand where Randi was having a small sundae and Tuna was eating a cone covered with rainbow sprinkles.

"I'm going, Randi," Kate said. "You coming?"

Randi gave her a strange look. "Uh, we came in my car, remember?"

"Then I'll walk," Kate said, and started to walk away. She knew she was acting like a baby, but sometimes that's what was necessary. Randi quickly said good-bye to Tuna and caught up to her.

"What's going on?" Randi asked. "And don't tell me you don't know and that you've never seen that Nick guy in your life."

"I *wish* I'd never seen that 'Nick guy' in my life," Kate steamed.

Randi trotted beside her and studied her for a moment. "He's the one, isn't he?"

"Huh?" Kate pretended she didn't know what her friend was talking about. But of course she did. Why did her best friend have to be so damn perceptive?

"Don't pretend you don't know what I'm talking about," Randi said. "Back over Christmas vacation. Mr. Mysterious. The lucky stud you did the deed with. You wouldn't tell me his name. No wonder. He's the son of your father's worst enemy."

Kate stopped in the middle of the parking lot.

"And he's the one from Bronson Park," Randi realized. "That night outside Club Che, with those two jerks who turned out to be from the FBI. Now I know why all of you were staring at him."

Kate hung her head and felt tears start to well up. It was so crazy. She'd cried more in the past six months than she had in the six years preceding them. She felt Randi's arm go around her waist. "It's okay," she said softly. "I didn't spend much time with him just now, but it was enough to tell that he's gorgeous and charming. And definitely worth spilling a few tears for. But what happened?"

Kate managed to blink back the tears. "What happened was,

he lied. There was another woman. For all I know, there's still another woman."

"Then why's he acting so interested?" Randi asked.

"Who knows? Once a player, always a player."

Randi glanced back at the boat show. "I don't know, Kate. I think I've seen the way players act, and somehow he didn't seem that way just now. But what do I know?"

"Let's just go, okay?" Kate said, not wanting to risk having Nick see her.

They went back to Kate's house and spent the rest of the day by the pool. Later they went to Shane Haslet's house to help him print the phony driver's licenses using the laser printer and laminating machine. When they got to Shane's, they found him and Adam Frost in the basement sliding the fake licenses into envelopes and addressing them. There were three stacks of envelopes on the worktable, each stack at least a foot high. Scattered elsewhere around the table were a couple of dozen colorful CD labels.

"Whoa, business must be good," Kate said.

"You won't believe it," said Shane, who was a skinny computer geek member of the FBLA with the world's largest Adam's apple. He gestured at the pile of envelopes. "This is one week's worth of orders."

"Amazing," Kate said, picking up a handful of envelopes. They were addressed to people in Michigan, Florida, Colorado, and California. "How do they all know about us?"

"MySpace," said Adam, a dark-haired brooding Bob Dylan fanatic. "It's spreading like wildfire."

"And thanks to Pay Pal, we don't have to worry about bouncing checks, phony credit cards, or any of those problems," said Randi.

Kate had to admit that when she'd first come up with the idea, she'd never imagined it being this successful. "So what about your parents, Shane?" she said. "Have they asked what's going on down here?"

"My parents are divorced, and my mom is a total technophobe," Shane said. "I told her I've gone into business making CD labels. All she knows is that I haven't asked for a penny of allowance in months. She brags to all her friends that I've become an entrepreneur."

"You have," Kate said, sitting down at the worktable. "So how can we help?"

Adam shoved the pile of envelopes toward her. "One of you can seal. The other can stamp."

They worked late into the night, printing, laminating, addressing, and sealing envelopes. Finally it was time to put them in the mail. As a precaution, Kate and Randi drove to more than a dozen mailboxes, spreading the letters around so as not to arouse any suspicions among postal employees as to why three or four hundred letters with the same return address would be in one mailbox.

It was nearly four in the morning when Randi dropped Kate back at her house.

"Feeling better?" Randi asked before Kate got out of the car.

"A little, I guess," Kate said. "I think I'll feel a lot better when I finally get to see Teddy again."

Randi gave her a funny look.

"What?" Kate asked.

"I don't know," Randi said. "I guess it's just hard to imagine two more different guys. I mean, that guy today, what's his name?"

"Nick."

"He's just so outgoing and dynamic and charming," Randi said. "And Teddy's just so unassuming. Like sometimes you don't even know he's there."

"Could be the difference between style and substance," Kate said.

"I guess," said Randi. "But why should substance have to win?"

"Because substance doesn't lie," Kate said.

Kate couldn't say she enjoyed the next three weeks of text messages and phone calls on the sly from Teddy while he was away on vacation with his family. But, thanks to all the things she had to keep her busy, they did go faster than she might have expected.

Finally the day came. Teddy IM'd her that he and his parents would be arriving on a flight from Madrid at one p.m. Kate practically counted the seconds all day. Each time her phone rang, she jumped with anticipation, then checked her watch and told herself it was too soon. The plane hadn't even landed yet.

When her phone rang at 1:13, her first thought was, *Could this be him?* But it was too soon. The plane would have just landed. They couldn't have even deplaned yet. She checked the number. It was totally unfamiliar.

Normally she would have waited to see if the caller left a message, but something told her to answer.

"Hello?" she said tentatively.

"Blessing?"

It was him! "Teddy! Where are you calling from? Whose phone is this?" Kate felt a rush of excitement.

"We've just landed," Teddy said. "The gentleman next to me was nice enough to let me use his phone for a moment. But I don't want to take advantage of his generosity, so I'll be quick. How are you?"

"Much better!" Kate blurted.

"Better?" Teddy sounded puzzled. "Was something wrong?"

What Kate had meant was that she felt much better that he'd called so quickly after landing. But she didn't want to tell him that. "No, no, I'm fine. How are you? How was the flight?"

"It was fine," Teddy said. "I'll tell you all about it later."

"Later?"

"I'll pick you up tonight at eight, okay?" Teddy said.

"What about your parents?" Kate asked.

"Never mind them," Teddy said. "Will you wear a dress?"

"Why?"

"We're going someplace nice," Teddy said.

"How nice?" Kate asked.

"Have you ever seen me in a jacket and tie?" Teddy asked.

"Wow, that's nice!"

Kate was beyond thrilled. It was so like Teddy to realize that she was upset about not seeing him for so long and to go out of his way to try to make it up to her. And what was that line about never minding his parents? Had he finally stood up to them? Had he finally told them that he was going to see her no matter what they said?

Kate spent the rest of the afternoon primping. Right on time, Teddy arrived in the promised tie and jacket. Kate suddenly found herself feeling shy and uncertain. They hugged and shared a brief kiss. Teddy seemed to understand and chatted about London and Ibiza all the way to the city.

He took her to a dinner club at the top of a tall building. It had a live band and an amazing view of the sparkling city skyline. They had a fabulous dinner and danced until their feet hurt. By the time they left, the streets of the city were empty except for some cabs.

On the way home they spoke less. Kate felt comfortable and held his left hand tightly in her lap. When Teddy protested that it would be safer if he kept both hands on the wheel, Kate said she was willing to take the risk.

Teddy drove to her house and parked in the circle. They kissed for a while. Kate was thrilled to be wrapped in his arms again. Earlier in the day she'd told herself that it might be best if things didn't progress too far at their first meeting. That it might be better to make him wait and rekindle his desire and passion. But now the idea seemed silly. She wanted him, and she knew he wanted her.

"Do you want to come inside?" she whispered huskily.

He seemed to stiffen and hesitate. A second later he backed out of their embrace. Suddenly Kate felt a terrible sense of foreboding. She gazed at him across the front seat of the Aston Martin.

"What is it?" she asked. "Is something wrong?"

The expression on his face said it all. He looked woeful, his eyes sad and mouth turned down. Suddenly Kate knew that something was wrong. She'd assumed originally that he'd taken her out on this fabulous date to make up for seeing so little of her that past summer. Now she sensed it wasn't about the past, but about the future.

"There's something you have to tell me, isn't there?" she said.

Teddy nodded.

"What is it, Teddy?"

He gazed at her with the saddest expression. "I just want you to be happy, Kate."

And in that instant, Kate knew she was about to become very, very unhappy.

11

THE NEXT AFTERNOON KATE TOLD RANDI ABOUT THE date while they bobbed on floats on the pool.

"I thought he wasn't allowed to see you," Randi said.

"He made a deal with his parents," Kate said. "Since they're sending him away to boarding school, he told them that it wasn't fair of them not to let him see me one last time."

"I thought he said he didn't have to go to boarding school if he didn't want to," Randi said.

"He thought he didn't," Kate said. "But he told me there were things he didn't know."

"Like what?" Randi asked.

"Like how people perceive his family business and how going out with me affects that perception," Kate said.

"In other words, going out with you hurts the business?" Randi guessed.

Kate nodded sadly. "That's what his parents say. It's what

they believe. It's just one of those stupid situations that's much bigger than the two of us."

"He's not breaking up with you, is he?" Randi asked.

"No. At least he says he's not," Kate said. "He just says we'll have to keep it on the down low this year. And then next year, when we're both away at college, it'll be different."

Randi gave her a dubious look.

"Please don't look at me that way," Kate said miserably.

"Sorry," Randi apologized. "But, seriously? Is that really the way you want to spend your senior year? Waiting for some guy you're not allowed to see?"

Kate shook her head.

"You don't have to, you know," Randi said. "Not with a hunk like—"

"Don't say it," Kate warned.

"Well?" Randi said. "It's true."

"I told you," Kate said. "Nick's a player. He's handsome, charming, and completely untrustworthy."

"Then maybe it's time to forget both of them," Randi said.

"I know," Kate said. "I'm just . . . I just don't think I'm ready to start all over again."

A week later, school started. Teddy went away, and once again Kate could only speak to him via IMs and phone. Day after day she felt as if she was going through the motions, pretending to be living in the present while all her emotions were on hold.

August ended, and September began. The air grew drier and

the mornings chillier. Kate spent most of her time with Randi, Shane, and Adam. Friday and Saturday nights were spent sitting in someone's basement or living room watching movies. When Randi mentioned that the community theater's final performance of the reprised version of *Guys and Dolls* was that Saturday night, Kate decided to go. Why not? With Teddy away at boarding school, she had nothing better to do.

Kate couldn't help laughing when Willy Shoes (who'd replaced Joey Buttons), Antoine, and Sharktooth Ray stepped on to the stage as the mobsters. Even more surprising—they were good! Just as Randi had predicted, all they had to do was act like themselves and they were very convincing.

The great thing about a community theater production of a musical was that the song and dance numbers didn't have to be well-performed, the players just had to be earnest. The awkward cornball dance numbers and off key song performances were wonderfully endearing. The audience laughed and cheered when they were supposed to, and sometimes when they weren't supposed to.

And at the end, they treated the cast to a well-deserved standing ovation.

After the show, Kate went backstage to congratulate Randi and the guys personally. A party was underway with soda (they were on school property) and snacks, and the original cast sound track of *Guys and Dolls* playing in the background. Kate found the three men standing in a corner next to a drum set and xylophone, speaking to a woman with short, curly red hair. The woman was wearing red heels and a red dress and while she was definitely attractive, there was something firmly businesslike about her. Kate had a premonition that made her heart suddenly ache. She stepped close enough to listen in.

"I know this business and I know the real deal when I see it," the woman was saying. "Hollywood wants authenticity, and you guys reek of that."

It was just as Kate feared. The woman was from Hollywood.

Meanwhile, upon hearing the word "reek," Willy Shoes's eyes darted left and right nervously. He dipped his chin down toward his shoulder and sniffed. The others gave him puzzled looks.

"Listen, lady," Willy said to the red-haired woman. "I'm sorry, but I showered this morning. It's just that it gets really hot under those lights. Any guy's going to sweat."

The others frowned and scowled. Kate stepped closer. "I think Willy's confused by the word 'reek,'" she said.

The guys and the redheaded woman turned. The guys smiled, and the redhead gave her a curious look.

"Hey, Kate!" Antoine said. "Did you see us? What'd you think?"

"I thought you guys were great," Kate said with a smile on her face and sadness in her heart. She turned to the redhead. "I think the thing you have to remember is that part of their authenticity is not having had the opportunity for a lot of education."

There wasn't a moment's hesitation on the woman's part. She got it right away. Kate could tell she was smart but she still didn't see how Kate could be connected to the guys. "And you are?"

"A good friend," Kate said, giving the guys a look that said that was all she wanted the red-headed woman to know.

The redhead caught the look. She didn't miss a trick. She offered Kate her hand. "Emma Hogkins from Creative Partners."

"Big Hollywood agency," said Sharktooth Ray.

"Talent scout?" Kate asked.

"We're a full-service agency," Ms. Hogkins said. "We scout, represent, manage, and do whatever else our clients need. I've just been telling your friends here that I think they could do very well in show business."

"Here on the East Coast?" Kate asked hopefully.

"There would be many more opportunities on the West Coast," Ms. Hogkins answered. "That's really where they have to go. Now that *The Sopranos* is over, a lot of people are trying to figure out how to do it again."

Trying to hide her sadness, Kate looked at the guys. "You're ready to go?"

As if they sensed what she was feeling, the guys gave Kate sheepish looks. Ms. Hogdkins continued to watch with a fascinated expression, as if she still couldn't figure out what was going on.

"Kate, girl, can you blame us?" Antoine said apologetically. "Ain't like there's much left for us to do around here."

"Except join Benny," said Willy Shoes.

"Benny?" repeated Ms. Hogkins.

Kate shook her head as if letting the agent know that Benny wasn't someone she had to be concerned about. But maybe that was the silver lining of the cloud. The guys might be leaving the organization, but at least they weren't going with Benny.

"I understand," Kate said. "You have to do what's best for you."

All three guys looked relieved. "You're not mad?"

Kate shook her head. "I only wish you the best."

Relief spread across the faces of the guys. "Thanks, Kate." "Yeah, you're the best."

By now, Ms. Hogkins looked absolutely fascinated. She took business cards from her small handbag and handed one to each of the men. Kate made sure she got a card too.

"As far as I'm concerned, I'm ready to start as soon as you are," Ms. Hogkins told the guys. "I know it'll take some time to settle your affairs here, so you'll call me and let me know when you're ready to come out west, right?"

"Definitely," said Willy Shoes.

An awkward moment followed, as if the guys weren't certain what to do next. Kate could almost feel the giddiness they were trying to hold back in her presence, when what they really wanted to do was celebrate. "Why don't you guys go get yourselves something to drink," Kate said.

The guys headed off toward the refreshment table. Kate turned to Ms. Hogkins and gave her a pleasant smile.

"You seem to have quite an influence over them," the agent said.

Kate nodded. "They're good, loyal men."

"Loyal . . . to?" Ms. Hogkins couldn't quite hide her astonishment.

"To me and my family," Kate said.

The agent blinked rapidly. She looked over at Willy Shoes, Antoine, and Sharktooth Ray as they furtively poured an amber liquid from a silver flask into their cups and then toasted. Then she turned back to Kate. "You mean, they're really . . . ?"

Kate nodded. "You said you could spot authenticity."

Ms. Hogkins gazed at the men again as if she'd surprised herself with her own intuition. "I had no idea. Truly."

"So I assume that your offer is legitimate," Kate said. "And that if they go to the trouble of traveling all the way out to the West Coast they'll be treated well and fairly."

The red-haired woman didn't respond as quickly or positively as Kate would have liked. "Well, it's show business. There are no promises. I can't guarantee anything."

Kate held up the woman's business card and added, "Please understand that if they do take you up on your offer, that won't necessarily be the end of their relationship with my family. You see, Ms. Hogkins, we've always taken very good care of our men."

The business card said that Kate had all the contact information she needed to find Ms. Hogkins if she felt the guys were being treated poorly. Not that she actually had the finances and manpower to go out to the West Coast, but Ms. Hogkins didn't have to know that.

In the meantime, the agent looked from the card to Kate and a little bit of the color drained from her face as she grasped what Kate was implying.

"Oh, I do understand," the agent assured Kate. "And I

promise you that we will give them the best treatment possible. And, on second thought, perhaps I can guarantee you that we'll have opportunities for them."

Kate smiled, pleased that Ms. Hogkins had taken her request to heart. *At least someone will have the chance to follow their dream,* Kate thought ruefully.

Across the room a door swung open and Randi and Mr. Brenner came in. The cast and crew began to applaud the coproducers. Randi beamed happily. Kate noticed that she was wearing a gorgeous embroidered teal jacket over an expensive-looking sheer silk blouse. And were those pearls around her neck?

Kate turned back to Ms. Hogkins and smiled. "I'm glad you'll take good care of my friends, because I look forward to hearing from them often. Now, if you'll excuse me?"

Kate headed toward Randi, who was surrounded by the cast and crew. All of them were thanking and congratulating her on the production and its success. Randi was flushed with pride and glowing in the adulation. Kate waited at the back of the crowd until everyone had gone.

"Congratulations," she said, giving Randi a kiss on the cheek.

"Can you believe it?" Randi gushed. "Another sold-out run! And it must have been word-of-mouth because we had unsold tickets right up until showtime and then they all went! We had to turn people away!"

"That's great," Kate said, happy for her friend.

"I bet you anything they're going to want to reprise it again for a week next spring," Randi said. "Derek says it's probably the most successful performance the community theater's every done. And part of the reason are your guys."

"I'm glad," Kate said. "Only, you may not be able to get the same cast next time."

Randi frowned. "Huh? Why not?"

Kate nodded at Ms. Hogkins, who was again speaking to Antoine, Sharktooth Ray, and Willy Shoes. "Hollywood agent."

"Serious!?" Randi gasped. "Kate, you can't let them go. I need them."

"I can't stop them," Kate said. "And I wouldn't even if I could. This could be a fantastic opportunity for them."

"And what about me?" Randi asked. "Don't I deserve an opportunity too?"

Kate couldn't believe what she was hearing. "You had your opportunity. You used those guys to help produce a successful show. Thanks in part to them, you've proved you can coproduce and direct. But you can't hold people back just for your own benefit."

Randi's expression became diffused with disappointment. Kate had to admit that she was surprised by her friend's apparent selfishness. She hoped that making a joke might lighten the mood.

"Looks like you're a victim of your own success," she quipped.

But Randi didn't appear to be amused. She glowered at Kate and said, "I just really didn't expect to see that success sabotaged so quickly."

"I don't see any reason for you to think it has," Kate said. "If you don't have the cast to do *Guys and Dolls* next time, you can do a different show."

Randi's response was a somewhat mysterious smile that was difficult for Kate to interpret. Kate didn't spend much time on it. She had other things on her mind. She dropped her voice and said, "There's something else I need to speak to you about."

Randi's forehead wrinkled. "Come again?"

"These are gorgeous threads," Kate said, tracing her finger over this sleeve of the teal jacket. "And are those really cultured pearls?"

"Oh, come on, Kate, they're nothing," Randi said. "Just a few baubles."

It was hard for Kate to believe that this was the same friend who, eight months before, had been wearing a dirty, torn, ill-fitting ski parka to school because she couldn't afford a real winter coat. And now she was calling a $400 string of pearls a bauble.

Kate lowered her voice. "Our fathers are supposed to be a couple of losers, remember? We talked about keeping a low profile so people wouldn't begin to wonder where all the money was coming from."

"There's nothing high profile about this," Randi protested. "Plenty of girls at school have them. Look at Brandy, Mandy, and Wendy. They all have them."

"Since when do we aspire to be like the BMWs?" Kate asked pointedly.

Randi's face hardened angrily. "Look, after the way they've treated me like dirt for all those years? I think it's more than justifiable that I might want to get some payback."

"That's your business," Kate said. "But not when it puts the rest of us in danger, okay?"

"I think you're making a little too much of this," Randi said. "We're not in *People Magazine*, Kate. It's not like we're being followed by fashion reporters who are tracking every outfit change."

"You'd be surprised," Kate said.

"Want to know what I find surprising?" Randi asked. "That my best friend apparently can't cope with anyone but herself being in the spotlight."

Kate was struck dumb by that.

"Give me a break," Randi snapped. "Don't play innocent with me. First you tell me I can't put on my first successful show ever again because you're letting those guys go to Hollywood. And now you tell me I can't wear nice clothes because it may attract too much attention. I think what's really bothering you isn't that it attracts attention, but that it takes the attention away from you."

Kate couldn't believe what she was hearing. "What are you talking about?"

"Oh, come on," Randi said. "Admit it, Kate, you've always been the queen bee in our relationship, and I've always been the poor cousin worker bee. Now all of a sudden the spotlight's on me and you can't stand it."

Kate stared at her friend like she'd gone crazy. "Are you feeling okay?"

"Oh, believe me, I'm feeling just fine," Randi said. "Better than I've felt in years. And why shouldn't I feel that way? For the first time in my life I look great and people think I'm a success. I guess it must be hard for my old friends to accept the new me, but hey, it's a big world out there and there are always new friends."

As if to prove her point, Randi turned away toward a group of people Kate didn't recognize. They must have been from the community. They welcomed Randi with kisses and words of congratulations and admiration. Randi turned back to Kate. The expression on her face said, "See what I mean?"

12

"**H**OW SOON DO YOU THINK YOU CAN COME UP?" TEDDY asked on the phone.

Kate felt her heart leap. This was just what she'd hoped she'd hear. "In a few weeks, I hope. I have the SATs this weekend and I promised my dad I'd visit him next weekend. So the weekend after that?"

"I don't know if I can wait that long," Teddy said.

"Neither do I," Kate said. "But what choice do we have? Unless you could come down here before then?"

"I wish I could, Blessing," Teddy said. "But I have a feeling my parents would know if I did."

"How?" Kate asked.

"This is a private boarding school. When people pay as much as my parents are paying, they can demand special favors."

"You think they have someone watching you?" Kate asked.

"I doubt it's anything that sinister," Teddy said. "There are a couple of security patrols that cover the campus in golf carts. My guess is that they've been told to keep an eye on my car and report to the head master if it's ever gone for a long period of time."

"Like a period of time long enough for you to meet me somewhere?" Kate said.

"Exactly," said Teddy.

"That's not very nice," Kate said.

"Like I said before, my parents are taking this more seriously than I could have imagined," Teddy said. "I don't know why, but I feel like I have to respect their wishes. At least, up to a point."

"And that point is?" Kate asked.

"I've come up here to boarding school because they wanted me to," Teddy said. "I won't come back home to see you because they don't want me to. But that doesn't mean I won't see you."

Kate appreciated the sentiment. She tried not to think about the fact that it meant that if she wanted to see Teddy this year, it would always mean going to him. After all, it wasn't his choice that he'd had to go away.

The following weekend she took the SATs, and the weekend after that she and Leo drove to the city again to see her father.

It was a crisp, early October day and the leaves were just beginning to turn yellow, red, and gold but had not yet reached their peak of color. Kate wore capris with a sweater. Leo sat beside her in the same old stained beige tracksuit he always wore. By now, Kate had given up trying to get him to change.

"I hear Antoine, Willy Shoes, and Sharktooth are heading out to Hollywood," Leo said as he drove his usual five miles per hour below the speed limit. "You really think they got a chance of making it in showbiz?"

"I think the agent who's going to represent them thinks that if anything bad happens to them, she's going to hear about it from the mighty Blessing organization," Kate answered.

Leo grinned, revealing a couple of the gaps where he was missing teeth. "Right. How would she know there's practically nothing left of the organization? You're a good girl, Katie."

"I'll miss them," Kate said.

"Yeah, me, too," said Leo. "You know, those three are probably your father's most loyal guys."

"After you," Kate said.

"Yeah, but I'm getting kind of old," Leo said. "Not much muscle. When those guys go, it's gonna be hard to keep the others from lining up behind Benny."

"I know," Kate said.

"You prepared for that?" Leo asked.

Kate gave him a crooked smile. "I'm not sure how anyone prepares for that, Leo. What about you?"

Leo shook his head. "I ain't prepared for nothing."

"How about going to Florida to be near your grandchildren?" Kate asked.

"That's what Darlene asks every day," Leo said as he drove. "If it's all falling apart, why stick around? Why not go see family while we still can?"

"And your answer is?" Kate prompted him.

"I can't leave your dad now," Leo said. "Not with him in the tank and the organization falling apart. He and I go too far back. He stuck with me through all kinds of crap. If I left now, with him in jail like this, I'd never be able to live with myself."

"What does Darlene say to that?" Kate asked.

"She understands, but she needs to be near the grandchildren," Leo said. "So I'm gonna send her down there. I told her I'll come down as soon as things get settled up here."

"That could be a long time," Kate said.

"Yeah, but she don't know that," Leo said.

"When was the last time you and Darlene were apart for more than a day?" Kate asked.

Leo shook his head. "Don't ask."

"Right," Kate said. "Have you two *ever* been apart for more than a day? I mean, since you've been married?"

"Hey, the one sure thing in life is change," Leo said a bit philosophically.

In the city, they parked in the same garage they'd parked in last time. But this time, even though it wasn't nearly as hot out, Leo grew tired walking and had to sit down to catch his breath. He sat on the corner of a stairwell with his hands pressed heavily on his knees as if he might topple over

"You okay?" Kate asked nervously.

"Yeah," Leo gasped. "I just gotta rest for a moment. I ain't been sleeping too good at night. It makes me tired during the day."

Kate could understand that. Given all the uncertainty, the slow death of the Blessing organization, and his worries about his wife and family, Leo was probably up half of every night worrying.

When he felt rested enough to walk again, they entered the correctional facility and went through the metal detectors and the tight prison security and into the visitors' room. This time Kate's father was already sitting there, waiting for them. Kate was surprised to see that he actually looked better than he had the last time she'd been there. He was clean shaven, his face had color, and he looked as if he might have even gained a few pounds.

"Hi, kid," he said.

"Hi, Dad," Kate said, feeling encouraged. "You look better than the last time I saw you."

"Some days are better than others," Sonny said. "Most of the time there's nothing to do except exercise, sit around, or sleep. So how can you not feel better after a while? How are you? How's Sonny Junior?"

Kate told him how her brother was still working weekends as a caddie. She wanted to keep the news light and good for a few moments before they got into the serious, depressing stuff. She was tempted to tell him about Amanda's alleged problems with Marvin the dentist, but decided that she didn't want to get his hopes up.

"So what's going on out there?" Sonny asked. "Brutus finished stabbing Caesar yet?"

The question wasn't as off the wall as it might have sounded. Kate knew her father was speaking in code. What he meant was, had Benny taken over the organization yet?

She shook her head. "Not yet."

"The visiting team start playing in the new stadium yet?" he asked. (Have the Blattarias taken over our territory?)

Kate shook her head. "Not completely. I'm not saying it won't happen one of these days, but so far we've managed to keep the hounds at bay."

Sonny raised his dark eyebrows as if he was sincerely surprised. "That's something, kid. I'm impressed."

"There's something else," Kate said. "Our three best dancing bears are joining the circus."

Her father scowled. Kate moved her face close to the Plexiglas and mouthed the names, Antoine, Willy Shoes, and Sharktooth Ray.

"Which circus?" Sonny asked.

"The distant shore," Kate said a bit obtusely.

Her father frowned, then raised both eyebrows in surprise. "La La Land?"

Kate nodded.

Her father half smiled and half smirked and shook his head. "Who woulda thunk it?"

"Of course, when they go, it's going to make things a lot easier for the visiting team to win," Kate said.

Sonny shrugged that one off. "At this point, it's not a big deal. All it means is the inevitable just became a little more inevitable."

"No offense, Dad, but aren't we being a little fatalistic?" Kate asked.

"That another one of those SAT words?" her father asked.

Kate nodded. "Basically it means you give up and just accept whatever happens."

"I get it," Sonny said. "So it's not like fatal as in it'll kill you. It's more like what's fated to be."

"Right."

"Can't argue with that," Sonny said.

Kate nodded uncertainly. She didn't quite understand where her father was coming from. While he wasn't exactly happy about the news, he didn't seem particularly depressed about it either.

"There's something you gotta do for me, kid," he said. "Those were the best trained bears I ever had. You gotta scrape together some fish for them. They deserve a good send-off."

Kate shifted uncomfortably in her chair. Her father had touched on a subject she'd been reluctant to bring up. But now that he'd brought it up, that was different.

"The refrigerator's pretty empty," she said.

"What about the freezer in the garage?" Sonny asked.

"It's empty too."

On the other side of the Plexiglas, her father pursed his lips and drummed his fingers against the desk. "I'm sorry to hear that, kid. I wish I had some more frozen goods for you, but that's all I had. But still, I'll really appreciate anything you can do."

"I know you will, Dad," Kate said, already formulating an idea in her head.

Kate assumed their conversation was ending, so she was surprised when he said, "How's your boyfriend?"

For a second she assumed he was speaking in code. Then she realized he wasn't. "Uh, okay, I guess. His parents sent him away to boarding school."

"Hmm." Sonny rubbed his chin thoughtfully as if this meant something interesting. But Kate couldn't imagine what it could be.

"Is there something you're not telling me?" Kate said.

"The walls have ears," her father replied.

Kate understood that the authorities listened in on these conversations, so there was little they could say. What she didn't understand was what there could possibly be about Teddy that would interest her father. The two had never met. Her father barely knew anything about him.

Kate made a confused gesture to her father through the Plexiglas. Sonny nodded back as if to say he understood and she shouldn't worry. But Kate still couldn't help wondering.

The next morning Kate got to school early and sat in her car in the parking lot. Each day the oranges, reds, and yellows in the trees grew a little brighter, and each day her own spirits grew a little brighter too. It was less than a week until she'd make her secret trip to see Teddy, and she couldn't wait.

Cars were starting to enter the parking lot. Kate watched and waited until Randi's Lexus showed up. Then she got out of her car and walked toward it. When Randi saw Kate coming toward her, she remained expressionless. The two friends had not spoken since the final night of the *Guys and Dolls* run when Randi had accused Kate of sabotaging her. In the days since, it had become clear to Kate that Randi had no intention of acquiescing to Kate's request that she chill her new infatuation with money and what it could do for a girl. Even this morning

Kate could tell that Randi's tight top and Coach handbag were new. In a way, she couldn't blame the girl. Having money was a new experience for her, and everyone knew money could change a person.

She just never thought Randi was one of those people.

"I need to talk to you," Kate said.

"Okay," Randi said, and locked the car, as if she expected that they'd speak on the way into school.

"No," Kate said. "Here, in private. In your car."

Randi scowled. "I'll be late."

"Not for the first time," Kate said.

"What's this about?" Randi asked.

"I'll tell you in the car," Kate said.

Randi looked around as if she expected to see thugs approaching her.

"There's just me," Kate said. "But please open the car. Don't forget, if it wasn't for me, you wouldn't even have that car."

Randi let out a big sigh and rolled her eyes, but she unlocked the car and they both got in.

"I hope this isn't about my clothes again," Randi said. "I have a right to spend my money any way I want."

"I need nine thousand dollars," Kate said rather bluntly instead of beating around the bush.

"What!?" Randi gasped.

"You heard me."

"Nine thousand is all we've got right now," Randi said.

"Okay," said Kate.

"But it's not yours," Randi said. "Part of it's mine, and part of it's Shane's and Adam's."

"I've already spoken to them, and they've agreed," Kate said.

Randi stared at her. "You're not serious."

"I am serious," Kate said.

"What do you need it for?"

"Some of the guys."

"What guys?"

"The guys in my father's organization," Kate said.

"But they have nothing to do with this," Randi said. "This is our business, not their's."

"They have *everything* to do with it," Kate said. "We're all in this together. That's the way the organization works."

"Whoa!" Randi put up her hands. "What are you talking about? I'm not part of any organization. This is just you and me and Shane and Adam."

Kate shook her head. "Anything that happens in Blessing territory is organization business. Anything that *I'm* involved in is Blessing business. There wouldn't even be a venture if it wasn't for me."

"Here we go again," Randi groaned. "You really have to get real, Kate. You've totally let this 'organization' thing go to your head. Like you're some kind of bigshot. Telling me what clothes I can and can't wear. Like whatever you say goes. But no way. Besides, everyone knows the Blessing organization is a thing of the past. Those guys did nothing to earn this money. And as far as I'm concerned, they're not getting a penny of it."

Kate leveled her gaze at her friend and said nothing. She didn't feel angry, just sad. Sometimes she felt like every friendship and relationship she had was affected by this world she lived in. The world of "organizations" and mobs. It was almost like being born with a handicap. It was something she'd had no choice about. Something she was just expected to live with. Randi crossed her arms and shook her head. "I'm sorry, Kate, but I'm not giving up a penny for those guys."

It was Kate's turn to sigh wearily. Even if they were fighting, she still thought of Randi as her best friend, but there were some things she really didn't understand. And it looked like it was time for her to start understanding.

"So that's that, right?" Randi asked.

Kate just shrugged.

"But you understand where I'm coming from?" Randi asked, as if she couldn't quite believe Kate was going to give up this easily.

Kate nodded.

"Still friends?" Randi asked.

"Always."

Randi pursed her lips. She leaned over and kissed Kate on the cheek. "Love you. Gotta scoot." They got out of the car. "You don't mind if I run, do you?" Randi said. "Don't want to be late."

"I understand," said Kate, who was in no hurry to get into school. "Go ahead. Catch you later?"

"Definitely!" Randi waved cheerfully and hurried ahead.

Kate watched her friend dash into school. Then she flipped open her phone and dialed a number.

"Yeah?" a gravelly male voice answered.

"I need you to do something," Kate said.

13

SCHOOL HAD JUST ENDED AND KATE WAS IN A CLASS-
room conducting the weekly meeting of the Future
Business Leaders of America. Today they were going to
have a debate and it was her job to start it off.

"Here's the question," she said. "Is it really possible for any
transportation company to be profitable and environmentally
friendly at the same time?"

A junior named David Welsh, who came to school every
day wearing cuffed pants, an oxford-cloth shirt, and a crewneck sweater, and who reminded her of Teddy in some ways,
raised his hand. "Honestly, I'd have to say no. Even biofuel
companies have to use a lot of coal or nuclear energy to produce their—"

He was interrupted by a loud knocking on the door. Kate
looked over and saw Randi waving frantically through the glass.
Tears were running down her face. Kate excused herself from the
debate and went out into the hall.

Her friend was dabbing the tears out of her eyes. "What did you do with my car?" she sniffed.

"Nothing," Kate said. "It's fine."

"Can I have it back?" Randi sniffed.

"Of course you can," said Kate.

"I'm sorry," Randi said. "I promise I'll never be a jerk again."

"So . . . you understand how it works?" Kate asked.

Randi nodded. "We're all one big happy family."

"No one's trying to be mean or difficult," Kate explained. "It's just how things work. Everyone shares. Remember your shearling coat?"

"Yes."

"We watch out for each other," Kate said. "Take the bad with the good and all those other clichés."

Randi grinned crookedly. "From now on, I promise I'll be a good gang member."

"*Organization* member," Kate corrected her with a wink. "It'll look better on your résumé."

That evening Kate picked up the money at Randi's house. Later she met Willy Shoes, Sharktooth Ray, and Antoine at Quik Nail and gave them each a plain white envelope with $3,000 in it. This was from her father, she told them. It was a going-away gift and a thank-you for all the years of loyalty they'd given him.

Willy and Antoine practically had tears in their eyes. They promised Kate that even though they were going to the West Coast, they would always be around to help her and her father in any way they could. Kate believed them. She gave each of them a hug and told them to stay in touch.

All week long, the only thing Kate could think about was getting in her car on Friday and driving to see Teddy. It was a beautiful ride—the trees were splashes of orange, red, and yellow—but the trip took close to four hours, and it was night by the time she got to the school. In the dark, there was little that she could see other than the silhouettes of rolling hills in the distance and the silhouettes of ivy-covered buildings with brightly lit windows.

Kate followed Teddy's directions to a residence hall whose brick walls were practically unrecognizable behind the thick layer of dark green ivy. As she turned up the drive toward it, her head-lights caught Teddy standing near the entrance, waiting for her. In classic Teddy style, he was wearing a light green cable-knit crewneck and tan cords, his blond hair falling down onto his fore-head. Despite the eagerness Kate had felt all week, she suddenly felt strangely anxious about seeing him. Perhaps it was just fore-boding and apprehensiveness. Would he still like her? Would they still be able to connect?

Kate parked. With a smile on his face, Teddy came around to the door, but for an instant Kate froze, unable to get out of the car. It had to be nervousness, she thought. She managed to release the door lock just as his hand closed on the handle. Teddy pulled the door open and the inside of the car filled with cool, fresh country air. Kate got out and Teddy hugged her. She still felt strangely unexcited, almost numb. But, why? Based on the last few times they'd been together, there was no reason to feel this way. What about the last night they'd spent together at the beach, making love on the sand? It had been so perfectly wonderful. Teddy had been so perfectly wonderful. And then that fabulous night of dinner and dancing in the city. Again, Teddy had been wonderful. Was it just the time apart that made her feel so cautious and uncertain? Or was it something more?

She hugged him back, and they shared a brief kiss.

"It's great to see you," Teddy said.

"You too," said Kate.

"How was the drive?"

"Easy. Your directions were perfect."

"Hungry?" Teddy asked.

Kate realized she was. "Yes."

"Come on." He took her hand. "We'll get you something at the canteen and then get you settled."

They walked along a path lit with lights on poles that reminded Kate of miniature old-fashioned streetlights. The scent of burning wood was in the air. Ahead was a low, slightly modern-looking gray concrete building. A sign beside it said STUDENT CENTER.

"This is the main student hangout," Teddy explained as they went up some steps and entered the building. In the lobby was a bulletin board with a variety of announcements neatly pinned to it. Kate stopped to look. Some of the announcements seemed typical of what one would expect at a school: an upcoming dance, a meeting of the drama club, a field trip to an art museum. But others were more unusual: a sign-up sheet for a Christmas vacation skiing trip to Switzerland, a request for volunteers to spend next summer building homes for the poor in Nicaragua, an exchange program with a school in Bangkok, Thailand.

Most of the student center was dark and closed. At first, the canteen appeared to be little more than a brightly lit room with some tables and a bunch of vending machines. But here, too, there were subtle differences: a microwave, a coffeepot, a selection of teas, a stack of plates with silverware and napkins. One of the vending machines offered fresh sandwiches, as well as tacos and burritos that could be warmed in the microwave. Another vending machine offered pie, cake, pudding, and other desserts.

Kate chose a burrito and a bottle of water. Teddy made a cup of Lemon Zinger for himself.

"So how are you?" he asked, sitting down across from her.

"Just happy to be here with you," Kate said. And that was true. She'd begun to relax and feel less nervous. But now that she was there, she didn't want to think about life back in Riverton.

"Me too," Teddy said. "I mean, not happy to be here with me. Happy to be here with you."

They smiled.

"So it looks like your parents finally got their wish," Kate said, looking around.

Teddy scowled for an instant, then understood what she meant and nodded. "Yes, I'm finally at boarding school."

"How is it?" Kate asked.

He shrugged. "Besides the fact that it's mostly filled with rich, spoiled kids who feel like they're entitled to the best of everything, it's okay. The classes are smaller, and there's more homework."

"How about socially?" Kate asked.

"It's a little bit isolated," Teddy said. "There are dances and sports events with other schools, but unless you feel like driving two or three hours on a weekend, there's no place else to go."

Even after they finished eating, they sat in the canteen and talked about school and parents and friends. Other students came and went, and Kate appraised them closely. Almost all seemed to fit into one of two categories: either preppy or a sort of pierced emo-hippie-grunge combination. Finally, Kate yawned.

"You've had a long day," Teddy said. "We'd better get you to bed."

They left the canteen. Kate couldn't help but wonder what Teddy meant by bed.

"I asked a friend of mine if you could stay in her room," Teddy said as they walked back across the dark campus. "Her roommate went to the Bahamas for the weekend."

Kate felt a small wave of relief. Despite what had happened over the summer, she knew she wasn't ready for any of the other possible sleeping arrangements. They got her bag from the car and headed for the women's residence hall. But Teddy stopped at the steps leading up the arching, ivy-covered entrance.

"I'm not allowed inside," he said, pulling out his cell phone. "I told Carter I'd call her when you got here."

Carter Constance Ochs-Burton wasn't *just* a girl, she was one of the most gorgeous creatures Kate had ever seen. She had long, straight blond hair, bright, friendly blue eyes, a cute little turned-up nose, and a perfectly proportioned mouth.

"Teddy's told me all about you," Carter said upstairs in her room after Teddy kissed Kate on the cheek and said he'd see her in the morning. Carter's room had yellow cotton curtains on the windows and her yellow bedspread said YALE BULLDOGS in big blue letters. She also had an easy chair with a blue and yellow YALE pillow.

"Oh, that's nice," Kate said, feeling a streak of jealousy rise inside as she wondered just how much time Teddy had spent speaking with this gorgeous creature.

Carter leaned closer and said in a conspiratorial tone, "I think he's very fond of you."

"And I'm fond of him," Kate said.

"You're a lucky girl," Carter said.

"Do you . . . see anyone?" Kate asked.

"Oh, not really." Carter smiled and hooked her blond hair behind her ear. "I'm so busy with sports and school. You know."

Kate knew, but still wished Carter had a steady boyfriend. They talked about which colleges they were applying to (Carter had her heart set on Yale—no surprise) and discovered by pure coincidence that they'd both visited the University of Pennsylvania on the same day the previous spring. By then Kate could hardly keep her eyes open, and they both went to bed.

In the morning, Teddy came by and they walked across the campus to the dining hall. With the sun up, Kate got her first real look at the school and its ivy-covered buildings, perfect green lawns, and green rolling hills in the background.

"This is more like a small college than a private school," Kate said.

"That's what everyone says," said Teddy. "And then the fathers always add, 'And it costs as much too.'"

"I bet it does," said Kate.

Teddy shrugged nonchalantly. Despite his obvious wealth, he never showed off about money. Breakfast was served buffet-style at round dining tables covered with table clothes. Perhaps because it was Saturday morning, hardly anyone was there. At one table half a dozen sleepy-faced girls sat in robes and pajamas, having not bothered to get dressed for the day yet.

"Is it so empty just because it's Saturday morning?" Kate asked.

Teddy nodded. "And some of the teams left after school yesterday for away-games at other schools."

"And let's not forget Carter's roommate who's in the Bahamas for the weekend," Kate added.

"There's always some of that," Teddy said.

It was a sunny, warm fall day and after breakfast Teddy showed her around campus and then took her for a hike to the lake, where they got into a canoe and paddled around for a while. They laughed and had fun together and the warm feelings she'd had for him in the past gradually returned. In the woods on the way back they stopped and kissed for a long time. By then it was time for lunch and they drove to a small town nearby and ate in a diner filled with grizzly-looking men wearing plaid shirts, dirty blue jeans, and base-ball caps. After lunch they went back to school and sat in the stands watching a lacrosse match and holding hands.

Around five in the afternoon, Kate went back to the residence hall and let herself in with the key Carter had given her. She went up to the room, kicked off her shoes, and sat down in the easy chair to rest. After a few moments there was a knock on the door and it opened. A girl with brown hair and wearing a pink cable-knit sweater stuck her head in. She scowled when she saw Kate.

"Is Carter around?" she asked.

Kate shook her head.

"Know when she'll be back?" the girl asked.

"Sorry," Kate said.

The girl frowned. "And you're?" she said, expecting Kate to fill in the blank.

"I'm Kate, Teddy Fitzgerald's friend."

Kate imagined that would mean nothing to the girl, so she was surprised when the girl's mouth dropped open. "You're the one!"

"Sorry?" Kate said.

"Oh." The girl covered her mouth with her hand as if she instantly regretted what she'd said. "Nothing. Sorry!" She backed away, and the door closed.

I'm the one? Kate thought uncomfortably, wondering what that meant.

She must have dozed for a while after that. Then the sound of the door opening woke her and Carter came in wearing gray sweatpants and a navy blue hoodie.

"Oh, sorry!" Cater apologized when she saw that she'd awakened Kate.

"No, problem." Kate yawned and covered her mouth. "I'm glad you woke me. I should be getting ready for dinner, anyway."

"Are you and Teddy going somewhere?" Carter asked.

"He said there's a nice place on the lake," Kate said.

"Oh, he must be taking you to Le Pernaise," Carter said. "It's a sort of pretend French restaurant, and the only place around here that serves anything remotely resembling decent food."

"I can definitely use a decent meal," Kate said.

The rooms were divided into suites so that each pair shared a bathroom. Kate took a shower. When she returned to the room, Carter was whispering on her cell phone. As soon as Kate came in, Carter said, "Okay, catch you later," and quickly snapped the phone shut.

For a second Kate had the paranoid sensation that Carter had been talking about her, but then she decided she was just imagining things. She started to get dressed. Carter sat down at her laptop and started IM'ing someone.

"So how did you and Teddy meet?" Carter asked.

Once again Kate had the strangest sensation. Carter simply didn't sound like the same person she'd chatted with about boys and college the night before.

"At school," Kate said. "Teddy used to go to the public school in our area."

"You lived near each other?" Carter asked. There was just the faintest tone of skepticism in her voice.

"Not far from each other," Kate said. "Why do you ask?"

"Oh, just curious," Carter said, as if she'd suddenly become self-conscious.

A little while later Kate went downstairs and met Teddy. The restaurant was very much the way Carter had described it—a sort of backwoods approximation of a French bistro. But the food was decent, and she and Teddy had fun.

After dinner Teddy wanted to go to a movie on campus. They drove back and walked to the auditorium. It was funny how, minute by minute, the more time Kate spent with Teddy, the more relaxed and comfortable and reassured she felt.

The school auditorium had comfortably padded seats, as nice as any movie theater's. People were filing in, chatting, saying hello to friends, and sitting down. Kate watched a group of girls go past down the aisle as they walked toward the front, looking for seats. One of them was wearing a familiar-looking pink cable-knit sweater, and Kate realized that it was the brown-haired girl who'd come into Carter's room earlier that day.

As the group of girls began to file into a row near the front, the girl in the pink sweater looked back at the crowd. Her eyes locked on Kate's for a moment, then she looked away. The group of girls sat down and Kate watched as the girl in the pink sweater leaned to the girl next to her and whispered something in her ear. The girl next to her glanced back at Kate, and then whispered to the girl next to her. Kate watched the process repeat itself over and over down the row, and then spread back to the rows behind like ripples spreading outward from a pebble thrown in water. The whispers, the twisting of the heads, the stares. This time Kate knew she wasn't imagining it. She glanced at Teddy beside her. He looked stiff and uncomfortable in his seat.

They know who I am, Kate thought. *They're brought up to be too polite to stare, so the fact that they're staring means it has to be something incredibly unusual. More unusual than just some girl who's come up to visit Teddy.*

Kate gazed back at them. Not with anger or resentment, but with a slight smile, as if pretending she appreciated the attention. The last thing she wanted to do was give them cause for more whispering.

The lights went down and the movie began, Kate tried to watch, but was mostly lost in thought. It wasn't hard to imagine how they'd found out. Not when there was MySpace. All it took was someone from this school to know someone who knew someone from Riverton. Next, Kate's thoughts turned to what would happen once the movie was over. There'd be more staring. More curious looks. And this wasn't going to do Teddy any good either. Did he really want to go through the rest of the year here being known as the guy who dated the daughter of the mobster?

Sensing the movie would end soon and the lights would go back on, Kate nudged Teddy and whispered in his ear, "We should leave now."

Teddy paused for just a second, as if his first thought was to wonder why she didn't want to stay until the end, but his second thought was to realize precisely why. He rose and slid out of the aisle. Kate followed. Even as they left, she could hear murmurs.

Outside in the cool, dark fall air, they walked without speaking for a few minutes.

Finally, Teddy said, "God, I'm sorry, Blessing."

"It's okay, Teddy," Kate said. "There's no way you could have known this would happen."

"I had no idea." Teddy sounded miserable and filled with regret.

"I know you didn't."

They were walking through the dark back toward the women's residence. By then Kate knew what she had to do. She knew Teddy would argue and that she would have to be strong and firm. And it would be best if she did it fast—before the others got back from the movie.

"I have to go upstairs and get my things," she announced. "Don't try to argue. I know what I'm doing. It's for both of us. It's for you because you don't want to spend the rest of the year here being known as the guy who dated the girl whose father was a mobster. And it's for me because there's no way I'm going to spend another minute here with all those people staring at me."

"Don't, Blessing," Teddy protested. "We don't have to stay here. We'll go somewhere . . . for the rest of the weekend."

She gave him a quick kiss on the cheek. "You're sweet, but I'm not checking into a motel with you." She reached into her bag and handed him her car keys. "Drive my car around to the back and meet me there, okay?"

Before he could argue anymore, she turned and hurried into the residence, knowing he wasn't allowed to follow. Upstairs she quickly gathered her things, then headed down and found her way to a back entrance. Teddy was waiting there with her car.

"Kate, I don't want you to—"

She pressed her fingers gently against his lips. "Thank you." She gave him a big hug and a kiss, then got in.

He leaned down to the window. "It's not fair. I can't tell you how sorry I am."

She smiled bravely. "Welcome to my world."

She started to drive and was just able to make it off the school grounds before she pulled off to the side of the road.

And burst into tears.

14

IT WAS ALMOST THREE A.M. WHEN KATE DROVE UP THE driveway and parked in front of her dark house. Despite how badly her visit to Teddy had gone, she was tired and fell right to sleep. She slept late, and would have slept even later if it hadn't been for the ringing doorbell downstairs. Kate sat up in bed puzzled. Whoever was ringing the bell had somehow managed to get past the driveway gate. She got out of bed and went to the window. Parked in the circle downstairs was Willy Shoe's white Cadillac.

Kate pulled on her robe and hurried downstairs. Willy, Antoine, and Sharktooth Joe were all standing outside. Despite the sadness she was feeling from the previous night, Kate managed to force a smile onto her face. "Hey, guys, what's up? I thought you'd left for Hollywood by now."

"You kiddin', Kate," Antoine said. "We wouldn't leave without saying good-bye first."

"So since today's the day, we came by to say so long," said Sharktooth.

Kate gave them each a hug. "You'll stay in touch, right? I want to hear about everything that happens with your new careers in show business."

"We promise you'll be the first to know," Willy said.

"When does your plane leave?" Kate asked.

"We ain't takin' a plane," Willy said. "We're driving out there."

"You're driving all the way across country?" Kate asked surprised. "Willy, have you ever been out of the state before?"

"Yeah, to the city," Willy said.

"Willy's never been in an airplane," Antoine said.

"And I don't see any reason to start now," Willy said.

"We got it all mapped out," said Sharktooth. "We're gonna go to Washington, D.C. to see the monuments. Then Memphis to see Graceland, then out to Santa Fe, and the Grand Canyon."

"With a little stop after that in Las Vegas to try our luck," said Willy.

"And from there to Los Angeles," Antoine said.

"That's fantastic," Kate said. "What an adventure."

"And we couldn't have done it without you," Willy Shoes said.

"Yeah, if you hadn't planned that video conference at school and introduced us to your friend Randi, this never would've happened," said Sharktooth.

"I guess you never know which way life is going to take you," Kate said. She thought they would agree cheerfully, and was surprised when her statement seemed to make them all become glum.

"Yeah, I guess not," Willy Shoes agreed.

ate looked at the men's faces. "Is something wrong?" she
d.

The three men traded glances as if trying to decide who should be the one speak.

"There's one other thing," Willy Shoes said. "And I'm afraid it's pretty bad news. We just found out ourselves last night."

"We couldn't leave without telling you," Sharktooth Ray added.

Kate decided to relieve them of the burden. "If you're going to tell me that Benny's finally taken over the organization, it's okay. We've all known it was coming."

Once again, the men traded uncomfortable looks. Suddenly Kate realized that wasn't the news they were going to tell her. It was something else. Something worse.

"What is it?" she asked, alarmed.

"You were right," said Willy. "It's about Benny. But he ain't just takin' over the organization. He's gone over to the Blattarias. He's delivered the whole thing on a silver platter."

The news took Kate's breath away. If Benny had simply taken over the organization, that always left the possibility that she and her father could someday take it back. But once the organization was in Joe Blattaria's hands, it was gone for good.

That was terrible news, and yet the men were still trading looks.

"Don't tell me there's more," Kate said.

Antoine nodded. "We feel like we got to tell you for your own good. Turns out Benny's been with the Blattarias for a long time. The whole thing with the Brink's truck robbery was a setup. They wanted us to grab the truck before they did so they'd have an excuse to go to war and take our territory."

Kate was truly stunned. "But the video conference."

"That was just an act," Willy Shoes said. "I'm telling you, Kate, we may be going out to Hollywood, but Benny's the one who really knows how to put on a show."

"And he's the one who told them about the factory?" Kate realized.

The men nodded. Kate was still stunned at how devious and backstabbing her uncle had been.

"Sorry, Kate," said Sharktooth Ray.

"Once we found out, we couldn't leave without warning you," Antoine said. "We had to let you know what you're up against."

Kate nodded. She didn't know what to think. All she knew was that this was bad. Very bad.

"Maybe you want to come with us to L.A.," Willy Shoes suggested. "You're a pretty girl. Maybe there's a career in acting for you, too."

Kate forced a crooked smile onto her face. "Thanks, Willy, but I don't think I can. I have to stay here and figure things out."

"Well, if you change your mind . . . ," Antoine said.

"We'll always have room for you," said Sharktooth Ray.

Kate felt the tears begin to well up in her eyes. What a bunch of sweethearts these guys were. She gave them each another hug and a kiss. Willy went last.

"If you ever need us," he said, "just call. We may be going to the other side of the country, but we'll be there for you."

"Even if it means driving all the way back," Antoine added with a wink.

Kate stood under the portico and waved as they drove away down the driveway. When they were gone, she turned around and went back into the house. The house she'd grown up in. But now that there was no longer an organization, how much longer would she be able to live there? And where would she go when she couldn't live there anymore? Her brother, Sonny Jr., was already sleeping on the couch at her mother's place. What was she going to do, share the bed with her mother?

Inside, a phone was ringing. Kate realized it was her cell phone, upstairs. She ran up the stairs and got it. "Hello?"

"Kate?" It was her mom.

"Hey, Mom," Kate said. She wished it had been Teddy, calling to say that everyone at school felt terrible about last night and wanted her to come back so they could apologize.

"Can you come to the hospital right away?"

Once again, Kate felt herself filled with apprehension. "What happened?"

"It's Leo," Amanda said. "He's had a heart attack."

When Kate got to the hospital, her mother was sitting in the waiting room with Darlene. Leo's wife was a heavy woman. Beneath the stiff hair and behind the thick makeup was a woman with a heart of gold. Kate hugged her and then hugged her mother.

"How is he?" she asked.

"They don't know yet," Darlene said. But behind her,

Amanda caught Kate's eye and slowly shook her head as if the outlook was grim.

"Can we see him?" Kate asked.

Darlene shook her head. "The doctor says he's resting."

Again, Kate glanced at her mom, who mouthed the word "unconscious."

"Do your kids know?" Kate asked.

"I don't want to worry them," Darlene said. "They got kids and jobs and too much to think about already. The doctor says the next thirty-six hours are critical. I figure I'll wait to see what happens and then decide what to do."

Except to go home, shower, and change clothes, for the next thirty-six hours, Kate, her mom, and Darlene stayed in the waiting room. They dozed on chairs and couches and waited. Sonny Jr. was sent to stay at his friend Tommy Swart's house. At mealtimes they took turns going down to the hospital cafeteria.

On the second day, Kate and her mom ate lunch together.

"What about school?" Amanda asked as she picked at her Caesar salad.

"I'm going to Randi's after school today," Kate said. "She's bringing home my books and assignments."

"Good," Amanda said. "This is an important semester, right?"

"It is if you're going to college," Kate said. "I've finished all my applications and sent them off. The question is, if I get accepted, do we have the money to pay?"

"We'll have to see," her mother said.

"You know about Benny?" Kate asked, holding one of the

french fries that had come with her hamburger. "I mean, going over to the Blattarias?"

Her mother nodded.

"It's all over, isn't it?" Kate said. "I mean, for the Blessing organization."

"Looks that way," Amanda said with a sigh.

"What are we going to do?" Kate asked.

Her mother gave her the strangest soft, dreamy look, then reached across the table and took Kate's hand in hers. Kate stared down at their clasped hands and back at her mom. *What in the world?*

Amanda just gazed at her daughter with that strange expression. Kate wasn't sure she'd ever seen anything like it on her mom's face before.

"Mom, what is it?" Kate asked, alarmed.

"Marvin's asked me to marry him," Amanda said.

Kate lost her breath. She stared back at her mother in disbelief. "And?"

"I told him I had to think about it."

"In other words, you're trying to let him down gently?" Kate asked hopefully.

Amanda looked surprised. "No. I meant, I really need to think about it."

That's what Kate was afraid of. First, her favorite guys leave for Hollywood. Then the rest of the guys become traitors and join the Blattarias, and now her mother was thinking about leaving her father as well. It wasn't quite the same as rats fleeing a sinking ship, but soon her father would have no one left except her and Sonny Jr.

"Uh, Earth to Mom, you're not even divorced," Kate said.

"That's not important," her mother said.

"What are you talking about?" Kate asked, wondering if her mom had lost her mind. "How can that not be important? Are you aware that there are laws against bigamy?"

"Your father is in no position to refuse," Amanda said. "He's facing a very long prison sentence. Possibly the rest of his life. He's not a vindictive man, hon. After all he and I have been through together, I know he'll do the right thing and give me an uncontested divorce."

"You're really serious?" Kate couldn't believe it.

"Hon, Marvin is a wonderful, generous man," her mother said. "And you know, it's not just me I'm thinking of. It's you and Sonny Junior as well. You both need a father who can be there for you."

"But Marvin's not my father," Kate said. "I don't want him as a father. Dad's my father. And as far as I'm concerned, he'll always be my father. Him and only him."

Her mother smiled approvingly. "Spoken like a good daughter."

"I mean it," Kate insisted. "I don't care what you do, Marvin's never going to be my father."

"Marvin is a very successful dentist," Amanda said. "He can pay for you to go to college."

Kate's sense of ire briefly grew, but then quickly diminished. In a way, this made sense. Her mother was probably scared. She probably had no idea of how she could continue to live in a manner to which she was accustomed. From that angle, marrying Marvin solved a lot of problems.

Kate smiled and leaned forward. She dropped her voice to a conspiratorial tone "So . . . you're thinking of marrying him for his money?"

"No! Of course not!" Amanda said, not taking the bait her daughter had offered. "All I'm saying is that marrying him would have added benefits for you and Sonny Junior. And think about your brother, Kate. He's at an age where he really needs a good male role model, not someone behind bars who's only available during visiting hours."

Once again, Kate felt like she was in a state of shock. "Mom, seriously, have you absolutely no sense of loyalty?"

Amanda's face hardened, and she withdrew her hand from Kate's. "That is so unfair. I left your father long before he got pinched by the feds. I've already served my time—twenty years while he chased every skirt in town. I have paid my dues, young lady. Twenty years of loyalty to him when he couldn't be bothered to show me an ounce of respect."

Kate might have disagreed, but she had to admit that her mother had a point.

By now, Kate had lost her appetite. She knew she had no right to be angry. College was a gift, not a right. For the past seventeen years her parents had given her a wonderful life.

And nothing lasts forever.

Mother and daughter left their lunches mostly uneaten and went back upstairs. Every few hours a doctor would come out to give them an update. Leo was still "resting." There'd been no change in his condition. All they could do was wait and see.

"Kate?" a voice said.

She looked up, and into the face of Nick Blattaria.

15

"**WHAT ARE YOU DOING HERE?" KATE ASKED, COMPLETELY** flummoxed and shooting a quick, nervous glance at her mother.

"I heard I could find you here," Nick said. "It might have helped if you'd check your phone messages once in a while."

Across from them, Amanda and Darlene looked up. Kate's mom gave her a look that said, "Who is that?"

"Mom, this is Nick Blattaria," Kate said.

All the BOTOX in the world could not stop Amanda's forehead from wrinkling. Kate continued to stare at him.

"Can we go somewhere and talk?" Nick asked.

Kate glanced at her mother, who shrugged.

"I'll be back soon," Kate said. The words were spoken to Amanda but aimed at Nick, to let him know that whatever he was doing there was completely inappropriate and she had no intention of giving him more than a minute or two.

She left the waiting room and began to walk down the

hospital corridor, not even sure where they were going.

"I hope you have a good reason for being here," Kate said. "Because otherwise, I can't think of anything that could be more disrespectful."

"Why do you think I'm here?" Nick asked.

"I honestly don't know," Kate said. "I don't understand how you even knew where to find me."

"Think about it, Kate," Nick said.

Kate thought, and the answer soon presented itself. Certain former members of the Blessing organization were now aligned with the Blattarias. But those former members still had ties to their old friends, and one of them was Leo.

"I'm here because I'm trying to stop my father from crushing you," Nick said. "He knows you've got nothing left. Your guys have either come with Benny and joined us, or they're off trying to be movie stars in Hollywood. He's taking over."

Kate was tempted to make up some crazy lie. Some bluff to make it seem like they still had something Nick and his father didn't know about. But she didn't have the stomach for it anymore.

"I assume you've known all along that Benny was secretly working with your father," Kate said angrily. "Or was that another thing your father kept from you?"

"I knew," Nick said.

"You see, Nick?" Kate said. "This is why I can't believe you. Half the time you claim you're telling me the truth, but the other half you admit you've either lied or withheld important information. So I never know what's going on."

Nick made a helpless gesture. "That's because we were on opposite sides before. And that's why I'm here. Because it wouldn't happen if we were on the same side."

"You're asking me to work for *your father*?" Kate asked in disbelief.

"I'm asking you to consider a merger," Nick said. "Turning the two organizations into one."

"Why?" Kate asked. "What do you need that for? Why not just take it all for yourselves?"

"There are certain people," Nick said, "people outside the organization, who are still loyal to your father. They say he treated them fairly. They're not sure they want to deal with us. It puts us in a position where we either have to force them to work with us or we can tell them the organizations have merged so they're really still dealing with the Blessings."

"But in a way, the organizations *have* merged," Kate said. "You've got the men, and the territory. What else do you need?"

A wry smile appeared on Nick's face. "Well, believe it or not, it looks like we need the Blessings' blessing."

"Even if we gave it, why should they believe you?" Kate asked.

"They probably won't," Nick said. "There's where you come in."

Kate looked at him like he was crazy. "You expect me to help you and your father take over my father's territory? Are you out of your mind?"

"I don't expect you to do anything, Kate," Nick said. "I'm *asking* you. Even my father thinks I'm crazy. He thinks all we need to do is break a couple of kneecaps and everyone will come around. But I'd rather not do it that way."

"Why not?" Kate asked.

"Because it's not my style," Nick said.

Kate eyed him suspiciously. "So let me guess what your style is, Nick. Bring me in to do spin control and reward me with another glorious night in Atlantic City before you vanish in the morning?"

Nick put his hand on her arm. "Chill, okay? I understand that you're tempted to become really emotional about this, but let's look at some hard facts. How are you doing financially?"

"That's none of your business," Kate said.

"Yeah, well, here's some business that might interest you," Nick said. "In return for helping us move into your territory, I've convinced my father to offer you a cut of all the income that results."

Kate's first inclination was to tell him she didn't believe him and that he could go to hell. But something told her that there was no harm in hearing him out. Nick hesitated while he read her expression. Then he leaned close and whispered a number in her ear.

Kate blinked with surprise. The number Nick had whispered was far higher than what she'd expected. "Why?" she asked, honestly bewildered.

Nick grinned. "Yeah, that's what my father wanted to know. I told him that's what I thought it would take. I had a feeling it would take less than that, but I didn't want to tell him."

"So I'll repeat my question," Kate said. "Why?"

Nick fixed his intense blue eyes on her. "Come on, Kate, you know why."

Was he saying he did it because he liked her? Because he was trying to mend broken bridges? People said talk was cheap. But they also said put your money where your mouth was. And Nick was doing that. Only, so far, it was still talk.

"I'm honestly touched by the offer," Kate said. "But forgive me if I'm not sure I should believe you. You haven't exactly been honest with me before."

Nick sighed and nodded. "As you never hesitate to remind me." He looked around and then gestured for Kate to follow him down the corridor to a supply closet filled with linens. Inside, he closed the door and then pulled a wad of cash out of his pocket. He quickly thumbed off twenty-five Franklins and held it out to her. "Let's call this an advance against future income, okay?"

Kate put her hands behind her back. "Keep your money. I haven't made up my mind yet."

Nick fanned the bills out. "You see how much is here?"

"Yes, Nick, I learned how to count in kindergarten," Kate said.

Nick gave her a begrudging smile and wadded the bills up. "As I've said before, you're tough. I like that." He was still holding out the money. "Suppose instead of an advance, you just take it as a gift? A friendly gesture. Couple of months ago you said talk is cheap. Maybe this isn't so cheap."

"You always give your friends large amounts of cash?" Kate asked.

"Just special friends," Nick said.

Kate shook her head. She might have needed the money, but there was no way in hell she was going to take it from Nick. "Sorry, not interested."

She stepped toward the door, but Nick blocked her path. "Come on, Kate," he said in a "let's be reasonable" tone. "Your whole crew has either quit or come over to us. Your organization's got no income. You must be living off some cash your father stashed away, but how much longer do you think that'll last?"

Kate felt the urge to blurt out that she didn't need his charity and that maybe she did have a source of income Nick didn't know about. But that would only tell him something she didn't want him to know.

"Nick, please step out of my way," she said. "I don't think we have anything more to talk about."

Nick didn't move. Instead, he stepped closer. "Kate, wait."

Kate stopped. A flood of memories came rushing back at her. How sweet and considerate he'd been the night they'd spent together in Atlantic City. How hard and taut his body had felt the time, a few months before, when he'd given her a ride home on his motorcycle. And how he'd taken her in his arms and kissed her the day he'd shown up at her house pretending to be the pool man.

Kate felt her resolve and anger start to melt away. This always happened when her proximity to Nick got too close. Her reactions to Nick and Teddy were a study in contrasts. With

Teddy, it always took time to warm up. With Nick, the heat was instant. Teddy was fun to be with (when there weren't other people around to ruin it for them). He was smart and gentlemanly and attentive and always concerned about her. Nick could also be gentlemanly and attentive, but that usually meant there was something he wanted. And yet, in a strange way, that made him alluring and a challenge in a way that Teddy wasn't.

Nick stepped even closer. Kate felt as if she was breaking loose from her mooring. Her thoughts got jumbled. She couldn't understand how he could have this effect on her. She felt his arms go around her. "I tried to tell you a couple of months ago," he whispered. "At your place. In the pool house."

Shut up and kiss me, she thought.

The door opened, and an orderly in blue hospital scrubs stepped in. When he saw Kate and Nick he was only momentarily surprised, as if this wasn't the first time he'd blundered onto a couple in the storage room. Almost apologetically he said, "Sorry, hospital staff only."

Kate felt her face grow hot and red as she and Nick left the room and returned to the corridor.

"You going back to the waiting room?" he asked.

Kate checked her watch. "Actually, I have to go to a friend's house. But first I'm going to say good-bye to my mom. Don't wait for me, okay?"

Nick frowned. "Why not?"

"I need to be alone and think," Kate said.

"Does that mean you're considering my offer?" Nick asked.

Kate held up her hand. "No pressure, okay? I'll let you know when I have an answer."

Nick nodded. Then, before she could stop him, he quickly leaned toward her and kissed her on the cheek.

She jumped back and made a face, but it was too late. Nick gave her a rakish smile and wink, and headed down the corridor.

Kate went back to the waiting room. She knew her mother was going to ask her what Nick wanted. But she decided it might be better not to tell her.

"What was that about?" her mother asked, as if on cue.

"Business," Kate replied tersely.

Amanda gave her daughter a curious look. "That's all you're going to tell me?"

"It's a long story," Kate said. "I'd love to tell you, but not here and not now. Besides, I thought you didn't want to be involved anymore."

Kate had meant it as the gentlest barb possible. Amanda raised an eyebrow as if to let her daughter know she'd gotten the point across. "Okay, maybe another time."

Kate gave her mother and Darlene each a kiss and then took the elevator down to the underground parking garage. It was crowded with cars and those thick square columns that she was always afraid of bumping into. She was looking for her car and spotted it next to a white van.

"*Kate!*" a voice hissed.

Kate felt a chill and quickly looked in the direction where the voice had come from. Nick was pressed against a concrete column as if he was hiding from something. He pressed a finger to his lips, then gestured for Kate to join him behind the column.

"What are you doing?" she whispered, keeping her distance and wondering if this was just a ploy to get her to squeeze close to him again.

"Watch," Nick said, and pointed at her car.

Kate frowned and looked. There was nothing to see—just her car, and lots of other cars. She had to wonder what Nick was up to. "What is this, Nick?" she asked.

"Keep it down," Nick whispered. "I was heading for my bike when I noticed something. Just watch."

Kate decided she'd give him another minute. Suddenly a head popped up between her car and the white van. It appeared that whoever it was had been doing something to Kate's car. She squinted and suddenly recognized the person.

"That's an IAD guy," she whispered.

"What?" Nick's dark eyebrows dipped.

"His name's Connors," Kate said, and explained how he'd stopped her outside her house one night a few months before.

The man swiveled his head around as if making sure no one was coming, and then ducked down again.

"That's no IAD guy," Nick whispered.

"How do you know?" Kate asked.

"Because the IAD investigates corrupt cops," Nick said. "They don't hang around parking garages going through people's cars."

"He showed me his ID and badge, Nick," Kate said. "It said 'internal affairs division.'"

"No way." Nick shook his head. "There's something else going on here. He came in that van, so my guess is maybe he's planting some kind of listening or tracking device in your car."

"Why?" Kate asked.

"I'll find out. Wait here."

But before he could go, Kate grabbed his arm. "Wait! What are you going to do?" she asked nervously.

"Take a closer look," Nick said.

Kate watched as he quietly slipped between cars until he reached his yellow motorcycle in the next row. He slid his helmet on and got on the bike. A moment later the roar of the engine echoed through the parking garage. Kate stayed behind the concrete column and watched as Connors' head popped up like a startled prairie dog on the lookout for hawks. When he saw Nick on the motorcycle he must have decided it was nothing to worry about because, once again, he ducked down beside Kate's car.

Nick took his time riding down the aisle, as if he were looking for a place to park. But just after he passed Kate's car and the white van, he stopped and put down the kickstand. With the bike still idling noisily, he quietly got off and walked back toward the van. Suddenly he moved quickly. The next thing Kate knew, there was a scuffle. All she could see were elbows and the tops of heads. It was impossible to tell what was going on.

Kate started to run toward her car.

16

WHEN SHE GOT THERE, NICK HAD FORCED CONNORS
down on his knees, twisted one of his arms behind his
back, and cupped his hand over the man's mouth.
Connors was making muffled attempts to yell, but little was getting through Nick's hand.

"You sure you know what you're doing?" Kate asked Nick.

Both Nick and Connors twisted their heads around to look at
her. When Connors saw Kate, his eyes widened. Nick nodded at
the van and said, "Quick, open the sliding door."

Kate did as she was told. The inside of the van was filled with
rolls of wire, and plastic milk crates brimming with microphones,
cameras, and other eavesdropping paraphernalia. Nick yanked
Connors up to his feet and forced him into the van. He told Kate
to get in with them and close the door.

Inside the van, Nick let go of Connors.

"You can't do this!" Connors gasped, pulling out his wallet and
flipping it open to the ID and badge. "I'm IAD."

Nick reached into his jacket pocket and pulled out a small black pistol. "And I'm Mr. Beretta. So shut up and put your hands on your head."

Connors did what he was told. Kate stared at the gun nervously. "Nick, if you're wrong . . ."

"I'm not wrong," Nick said. "Open the wallet."

The wallet was a dual-fold and opened to the IAD ID and the badge. She showed it to Nick. "See?"

"Now check his driver's license," Nick said.

"You can't do this!" Connors sputtered.

Nick aimed the gun at him. "I'd quiet down if I were you."

Kate found the driver's license. It had Connors' photograph, but a different name.

"Rudolph J. Prentiss?" Kate said.

"Rudolph," Nick said with an amused grin. "How's the North Pole?"

"I don't know what my parents were thinking," Rudolph, formerly known as Connors, muttered with a shrug. "Thanks to them, I have to go through life with everyone calling me Red Nose and asking how the other reindeer are doing."

"I assume you prefer Rudy?" Nick asked.

"RJ," he said.

"Okay, RJ, so what's the story?" Nick said. "What were you doing to my friend's car?"

RJ twisted his head around at all the electronics gear in the van. "You have to ask?"

"Where is it?" Nick asked.

"Under the passenger seat," RJ said. "Look, since you're gonna take it out, how about giving it back, okay? Those suckers cost me almost two hundred bucks each."

"Sorry, RJ," Nick said. "Guess you'll have to write it off as a business loss."

RJ's shoulder's sagged, and he shook his head woefully.

"Who do you work for?" Kate asked him.

RJ smirked at her. "You gotta be kidding."

Kate glanced uncertainly at Nick, who shrugged indifferently.

"Look, you caught me, okay?" said RJ. "You'll get rid of the bug and I'll make up some excuse about why I couldn't complete the job. That's the end of it." He turned to Nick and nodded at the gun. "So how about putting away the cannon, okay, bigshot? Nobody's shooting anybody over a stupid bug."

Nick slid the gun back into his jacket. RJ took his hands off his head and checked his watch. "Listen, I don't mean to be rude or anything, but I gotta pick up my daughter at day care. I was late yesterday and if I'm late again today, my wife really will shoot me."

Nick didn't budge. "Just one last thing," he said, and tilted his head toward Kate. "You never bother her again. Stay away from her house and car and everything else."

"I hear you," RJ said.

Nick slid open the van's door, and he and Kate got out. The white van backed out of its spot and drove away.

"Why didn't you press him harder on who he worked for?" Kate asked Nick.

"Because it wouldn't mean anything," Nick said. "People who hire guys like that know there's a chance the guy might get caught. So they have intermediaries who do the hiring for them. RJ doesn't have a clue who he's really working for."

"But you're sure it's not the police or the FBI?" Kate asked.

"Almost positive," Nick said.

"Maybe your father did it without telling you?"

Nick shook his head.

"I just can't imagine who else would want to bug my car," Kate said.

"Can't help you there," Nick said. He opened the passenger-side door to her car, then kneeled down and felt around under the seat. Kate watched as he yanked hard on something and stood up. In his hand was a disc about the size and thickness of a wristwatch, and a wire about a foot long. "Want it?"

Kate shook her head. Nick dropped the bug to the garage floor and crushed it with his heel. He looked up at her, and their eyes met.

"Thank you, Nick," Kate said.

"You're welcome."

Kate felt that magnetism drawing her toward him again. It was ceaseless and always tempting.

"Kate," Nick said, and she instantly knew he was going to start coming on to her again.

"Don't," she cut him short. "Please, Nick, give me a break. Not now."

Nick frowned, but nodded. Strangely, part of Kate felt

disappointed. As if that part of her wanted him to keep trying. It was so obvious that she was torn. But right now she needed a break. Nick spread his arms the way a friend does when he or she wants to give you a friendly hug. Kate hesitated, surprised by this gesture that was clearly meant to be more of warmth than lust. She nodded and felt his arms go around her.

"Take care of yourself, okay?" he said.

Kate nodded and felt her defenses collapse faster than an overpowered army's. Nick sounded completely sincere, as if he really did care. But just when she would have stayed in his arms, he let go and backed away toward his motorcycle. "Catch you later."

Kate nodded. She couldn't ever remember feeling more emotionally conflicted or confused.

She was driving home when a text message from Teddy appeared on her phone. "Pay Phn. ASAP."

That was strange, but Kate was passing a multiplex and knew there'd be pay phones inside. She parked and went into the popcorn-scented air. She texted Teddy back that she'd found a pay phone. Teddy texted her a phone number. Kate used the pay phone to call it. Clearly he was worried about phones being tapped.

"Hi, Blessing," he said. "How are you?"

"I'm fine, Teddy, how about you?" Kate asked. "Anyone giving you grief about the mobster's daughter?"

"I actually think it's bought me some cachet," Teddy said. "I'm now a cool, dangerous, preppy gangsta who hangs out with a certain underworld element."

"Glad I could be of some assistance," Kate said. "But you didn't want me to call you just so you could tell me that, did you?"

"No, but believe it or not, it does have something to do with why I'm calling," Teddy said, sounding serious. "You won't believe this, Blessing, but my parents discovered that their phones have been tapped."

"Why?" Kate asked.

"They had some people look into it and it appears that it's because there are records of phone calls between my house and your house."

"Oh, God, I'm sorry, Teddy," Kate said.

"They're completely crazed over it," Teddy said. "My father especially. Just between you and me, I can't figure out what the big deal is. At this point, it can't really be a big surprise, you know?"

"I'm sure it's just the feeling that their privacy's been invaded," Kate said.

"Could be, but whatever it is, they've just gone over the edge," Teddy said. "I've never seen them like this. They . . ." He hesitated for a moment. Suddenly Kate sensed there was something more.

"What is it, Teddy?" Kate said.

"They found out you came up here," Teddy said. "I've never seen them go so ballistic."

Kate began to get a sick feeling inside. Was he breaking up

with her? "But you've always said you didn't care what they thought."

"It's not that, Blessing," Teddy said. "It's the effect my actions have had on them. I've never done anything before that really had a negative impact on their lives. They might not have been happy that I didn't go to boarding school, but it was easy to explain to their friends that I was just being rebellious. Besides, I always made the honor roll and did all the extracurricular stuff. But this is different, Blessing. My actions have had a seriously negative impact on their lives and on business. It's not fair to them. This isn't just a matter of something being embarrassing in their social set. This has harmful implications to a business that three generations of Fitzgeralds have dedicated their lives to building."

Kate could hear the gravity in his voice. This had a seriousness that probably few people could understand unless they were part of a one-hundred-year-old family business worth many millions of dollars. But when you looked at it from that perspective, it did seem horribly unfair to jeopardize so many decades of hard work and sacrifice.

"I do understand, Teddy," Kate said. "Really, I do. It's not fair to them."

"Thanks, Blessing, I appreciate hearing that from you," Teddy said.

The phone line grew quiet. Kate could hear the faint sounds of other calls. "So . . . what does that mean?" she finally asked. "I mean, for us?"

"Uh . . . I don't know," Teddy said, sounding as if he truly hadn't thought about it.

"Well, it can't be good, can it?" Kate asked, feeling a gloom descend around her.

"No, I guess not," Teddy said, as if the gloom on his end was deepening as well.

"Is . . . there something you want to tell me?" Kate asked.

"Huh?" The question seemed to catch Teddy by surprise. "Oh . . . uh, no! Absolutely not. I just wanted to tell you about the phone taps. I mean, because I thought you should know. That's all, Blessing. Really."

Kate felt relieved. So he wasn't calling to break up with her.

"I mean, I guess it wasn't like you were going to come back up here anytime soon again, anyway," Teddy said. "But I'm worried that it might be a little harder for me to see you even when I'm at home."

Kate didn't see how it could be any harder than it already was, since his parents had already made it nearly impossible for them to see each other there in Riverton. So, while he wasn't breaking up with her, he *was* saying that it would be even harder to see her, which basically meant impossible. Perhaps they could become pen pals? *What I wouldn't do for a little good news right now,* Kate thought woefully.

"But you still *want* to see me, don't you?" she asked.

"Of course I do," Teddy said. "That's not what this call is about. I just thought you should know what's going on."

Over the phone Kate heard sounds in the background, as if a

door had opened and shut. This was followed by bits of muffled conversation, making Kate wonder if Teddy had put his hand over the phone's mouthpiece.

"Teddy?" she said.

There was no answer. Just more muffled sounds. Kate thought for a moment that she heard a girl's voice.

"Teddy?" she said once more.

Still no answer. Kate wasn't certain what to do. Then Teddy came back on again, but as a whisper. "Kate, you still there?"

"Yes," Kate said. "Teddy, where are you?"

"Carter's room," he said in a low voice. "I had to find a safe phone. My parents get my monthly phone bills with a complete record of incoming and outgoing calls, so the only other way to speak to you now is to use a phone in someone else's room."

"But I thought guys weren't allowed in the girls' dorm," Kate said.

"They're not," said Teddy. "She snuck me in. But I have to go now. Someone might be coming. Talk to you soon, okay?"

"Yes," Kate said.

The line went dead. Kate hung up the pay phone and felt her mood darken even more. That was probably even more bad news than Teddy had intended. Kate wasn't sure which upset her more: the news that it would be even harder to see Teddy, or the news that he'd been in that beautiful girl's room.

Kate left the multiplex and was walking back to her car when her cell phone began to ring. Hoping that it was Teddy calling back, she eagerly dug it out. It was Randi.

Kate almost answered, then decided not to. She really didn't feel like speaking to anyone right now. She'd let Randi leave a message and then she'd check it later.

But no sooner had the phone stopped ringing than a text message from Randi came across: "Huge trouble! Help!"

17

KATE COULDN'T BELIEVE IT. JUST WHEN SHE'D THOUGHT nothing worse could happen, now this. She considered pretending she hadn't yet read Randi's text message. At least, not for the next few hours while she tried to digest the latest bad news from Teddy.

But Randi was her best friend and had been there for her long before Teddy had come along. And despite their recent differences, it just wasn't in Kate's nature to ignore a plea for help.

As soon as she got into the car she dialed Randi's number.

"Kate!?" Randi practically screamed. "You won't believe what those subhuman scabs are doing! They're blackmailing—"

As soon as Kate heard the word "blackmail," she cut the conversation off. "Not on the phone."

"We have to talk, pronto," Randi said. "Can I come to your house?"

"No!" Kate gasped. With all the talk of wiretapping, not to mention finding Rudolph the red-nosed bugger messing with her car, she was feeling totally paranoid. "Meet me at the high school track."

"You're not going to make me run with you, are you?" asked Randi, who hated all forms of exercise.

"No, we'll walk. And listen, you got my books and assignments, right? Don't forget to bring them."

Twenty minutes later they were walking around the high school track.

"Why are we doing this?" Randi asked.

"In this business they call this a walk-and-talk," Kate explained. "As long as we're walking like this we can see who's around us and make sure they're not listening in. They can't plant any bugs anywhere because we won't stay in one place. And even if someone's hiding somewhere with a shotgun mike, they'd only be able to pick up bits and pieces of the conversation."

"What if they've got a lip-reader with binoculars?" Randi asked half seriously.

"I don't think that would be admissible in court," Kate said. "May I say that for a girl who sounded totally panicked a little while ago, you're acting awfully calm."

"Inside, I'm still freaking out," Randi assured her. "It's just not my thing to show it for long."

This was true. "So what's the story?" Kate asked.

"Stu and Tanner are blackmailing me," Randi said. "Or, since it's also your money, I guess I should say, they're blackmailing us."

Kate stared at her in disbelief. "You can't be serious."

"I wish I wasn't," Randi said. "They want five thousand dollars or they're going to tell the police what we're up to."

"Then we'll just shut down, erase the hard drives, and get rid of all the evidence," Kate said.

Randi shook her head sadly. "Too late. They already have the evidence."

"How?"

"About a week ago, some kid showed up," Randi said. "He claimed he went to Munson and he needed a fake driver's license right away. For that night. Shane and I had our doubts, but the kid was desperate. He even offered us twice what we usually charge. So we figured what the heck and did it on the spot."

"You think he was wearing a wire?" Kate asked.

Randi nodded slowly. "He acted really interested. Kept asking questions about how we did it and where we got the materials. Shane and I probably said more than we should have. And the whole time he kept looking over our shoulders and talking about what we were doing as if he was narrating."

Kate felt a chill. "Don't tell me he was wearing a hat."

"You got it. Not just a hat. A baseball cap. And you know that stupid style where guys wear the sunglasses on the top of the brim? He could have so easily had a little camera in there. I mean, think about how thin the camera in your cell phone is."

"Believe me, I'm aware of how they work," Kate said. "So we have to assume Stu and Tanner have evidence. But it's such a crappy thing to do. How do we know they're really going to do it and it's not just a bluff?"

Randi stared at the ground, and her shoulders sagged as if under some invisible weight. "Can you spell shrinkage?"

"Oh." Kate had momentarily forgotten.

"Maybe doing that video wasn't such a great idea," Randi said regretfully.

"Wait a minute," Kate said. "You only did that video because of the video they did of you. Why is it okay for them to do one of you but not for you to do one of them?"

"It wasn't," Randi said. "But look at the problem we have now. We don't even have five thousand dollars."

And if we did, we sure wouldn't give it to those two jerks, Kate thought. So what would they do? Back when her father was running the organization—back when there *was* an organization to run—the answer would have been simple. Her father would have sent a couple of his guys from the crew to pay a "visit" to Tanner and Stu, and that would have been the end of the problem. Not that the guys would have hurt the boys. They wouldn't have had to. All they would have had to do would be take the boys for a ride in the backseat of a car and explain that if they ever bothered Kate and Randi again, they were liable to suffer an "accident" that might result in a broken arm or leg. There was little doubt in Kate's mind that Tanner and Stu would spend the rest of their time in high school afraid of their own shadows.

But without the crew and the Blessing organization behind her, what could she do?

When the answer came to her, she didn't like it. But she knew she didn't have a choice.

"What are we going to do?" Randi asked anxiously.

"Give me a moment," Kate said. She wanted to think this out clearly. They would have to pretend to agree that they were going to pay the blackmail. And then they would have to lure Stu and Tanner to an isolated place, but it couldn't be obvious or the boys would suspect a trick and refuse to go.

They were still walking around the high school track. As they came around the bend, Kate glanced toward the school entrance. Near it was the big orange wooden sign that went up every year that announced the annual Halloween fair.

"What about the Scare Fair?" Kate asked.

"What?" Randi said. "Earth to Kate. Who cares about a stupid fair? We've got a major crisis on our hands."

"I know," Kate said. "We'll tell Stu and Tanner we'll give them the money at the fair."

"Hello? Didn't you hear what I just said?" Randi said. "We can't do that. The Scare Fair's tomorrow night and I just told you we don't have—"

"I know what you told me," Kate said. "But just do it, okay? Call the boys and tell them we'll meet at the fair. Then call me back and tell me what they say."

"I hope you know what you're doing," Randi said.

That makes two of us, Kate thought.

They walked back to the parking lot and got into their cars. But while Randi drove away, Kate opened her phone and dialed Nick's number.

"Yeah?" Nick answered gruffly.

"It's Kate."

"Oh, hi." He softened his voice.

"So, I'm curious," Kate said. "Do you always sound so gruff on phones because you think you have to sound that way for the crowd you usually deal with?"

"What do you think?" Nick asked.

"I think you do."

"Just don't tell anyone," Nick said. "So what's up?"

"Can we meet?"

"Wow, that was fast . . ."

"It's not what you think," Kate said.

"With you, it never is."

Kate resisted the temptation to ask what he meant by that.

"So, uh, where do you want to meet?" Nick asked.

Kate hadn't eaten since lunch and was starving. But she didn't want to give Nick any misleading ideas. This was strictly business. "It doesn't matter. It's just for a quick drink."

"Of course," Nick said. "But still, some place private where we can talk?"

Kate immediately understood what he was implying. "Yes, right. Exactly."

"Where are you?"

"The high school."

"Give me ten minutes," Nick said, and hung up.

Kate closed her phone and almost reflexively flipped down the vanity mirror behind the sun visor and reached into her bag for her makeup. Whoa! What exactly was she doing? Since when did she want to look good for Nick? This was business, wasn't it? On the other hand, it was natural to always want to look nice, wasn't it?

Kate instinctively knew that she was having a conversation with herself that wasn't going to be resolved, so she primped on principle.

Twenty minutes later, Nick's silver Mercedes rolled into the parking lot. Kate was glad he hadn't come on the motorcycle. She didn't feel like dealing with helmet hair. Whereas Teddy would have hopped out and opened the door for her, Nick waited for her to get in herself. When she did, Kate couldn't help noticing that he'd changed clothes from earlier and was now wearing a nice dinner jacket.

"Where are we going?" Kate asked as he drove out of the school lot.

"A little place I know," Nick said. "How's your friend in the hospital?"

"Oh, Lord!" Kate had been so distracted by Teddy and Randi that she'd forgotten. She immediately pulled out her phone and dialed Darlene's number.

"How is he?" she asked when Leo's wife answered.

"Better!" Darlene answered excitedly. "The doctor said he's responding."

"That's great," Kate said. "I'll see you tomorrow, bright and early, okay?"

"Shouldn't you go back to school?" Darlene asked.

"I'm on top of it," Kate said. "A friend of mine is bringing all the assignments so I can keep up."

"Okay, see you tomorrow."

Kate closed the phone. Nick glanced at her. "Sounds like he's doing better?"

"Yes," Kate said.

"Good," Nick said.

"Do you really care?" Kate asked.

"He's someone you care about, so I care," Nick said.

"That sounds like a line," Kate said.

"To you, everything sounds like a line," Nick said.

"Well, admit it, Nick," Kate said. "You've told me a few before."

Nick gave her an exasperated look. "And how many times are you going to remind me?"

Kate knew he had a point. Maybe it wasn't him she was reminding. Maybe it was herself. She had to be careful.

They pulled into a parking lot for a health gym, liquor store, and dry cleaner. Nick started to get out of the car, so Kate did the same.

"Let me guess," she said, glancing at the gym. "You need to work up an appetite first?"

Nick pointed at something she hadn't noticed—a small, white, shoe box–shaped building that stood alone just beyond the health gym. The building had no sign, and the front door and window were covered with black curtains. And now Kate noticed something else: Parked in the corner of the parking lot closest to the building were a collection of large, new, black Mercedes-Benzes.

"Ah, I see," she said.

They walked to the front door. This time, Nick opened it and held it for her.

The first thing Kate noticed when she walked in was the smell of cigarette and cigar smoke. It wasn't horribly overpowering, but you couldn't miss it. This seemed odd, since state laws demanded that restaurants be smoke-free.

Two dark-haired men in black jackets standing just inside the door seemed to tense slightly when Kate came in, but they quickly relaxed when Nick followed.

"Hey, Nick, wuzzup?" They greeted him with handshakes and pats on the back and then turned again to appraise Kate.

"This is my friend, Kate Bl—ahem!" Nick had begun to say Kate's last name, but then pretended to cough.

Both guys nodded as if Bl—ahem were actually her real last name. Then one of the men checked his watch and scowled. "Sorry, Nick, the kitchen ain't open yet."

Kate glanced around the restaurant. It was unusually dark, but she could see men—not a woman in sight—seated at some of the tables with glasses or espresso cups in front of them.

"We're here for a drink," Nick said.

"Oh, no problem," one of the men said, and gestured to the bar.

Nick and Kate sat. Kate slid the glass ashtray away from her and raised a quizzical eyebrow toward Nick.

"I know what you're thinking," Nick said. "This isn't actually a restaurant. It's more of a private club. And therefore it can make its own rules. So, uh, before we get down to whatever the business is, how are you?"

"Fine," said Kate.

"Do you mind if I tell you that you look tired?" Nick asked.

Kate shook her head. If she looked tired with makeup, she must have looked *really* tired without it. Meanwhile, one of the men stepped around to the inside of the bar as if to take their order.

"How about something that'll relax and wake you up?" Nick suggested.

"Sounds perfect," Kate said.

Nick ordered two Spanish coffees. The bartender left the bar and disappeared behind a curtain at the back of the dining room.

"So, I'm curious why you didn't mention my last name?" Kate whispered. "Are we in enemy territory?"

Nick grinned. "Not anymore."

This was true. Now that Benny had taken the remaining members of her father's organization and joined with the Blattarias, there was no enemy territory.

"But, seriously?" Nick said in a low voice. "I'd prefer my father didn't find out I was here with you."

"Can I ask why?" Kate asked.

"Let's just say that there are still some bad feelings," Nick said. "It'll pass with time."

The bartender returned with two cups of steaming coffee and placed them on the bar, then poured liquors from several different bottles into them. Kate inhaled the combination of coffee and alcohol. "That smells fabulous."

"Try it," Nick said, taking a sip.

Kate did. She wasn't sure she'd ever tasted anything like it before. The only word she could think of to describe it was exotic. "What's in it?"

"Espresso, rum, and Tia Maria."

Kate took another sip and felt it warm her.

"So what's on your mind?" Nick asked.

Kate's eyes darted at the bartender. Nick understood. "Hey, Sammy, we need a little privacy."

The man nodded and moved away to a table near the entrance. Nick turned to Kate and leaned close.

"I'm being blackmailed," Kate said.

Nick frowned. "Why?"

"I'd rather not say," Kate said, not wanting him to know about her venture with Randi. Now that the Blattarias were taking over Blessing territory, they would expect a cut of all illegal activities. That wasn't something Kate necessarily wanted to give up.

"Okay . . . so why are you telling me this?" Nick asked.

"I need your help," Kate said.

"You need my help, but you won't tell me why," Nick said.

"I told you why," Kate said. "I'm being blackmailed."

"Right." Nick slowly nodded. "Now, you know this is exactly the kind of thing I've been talking about. If you'd join us, you wouldn't even have to ask me. You could just tell a couple of the guys to go bang some heads."

"I'm still thinking about it, Nick," Kate said. "Really, I am. But this isn't the right time. There are too many other things going on."

Kate took another sip of the Spanish coffee. As Nick had promised, it both perked her up and relaxed her. Now she became aware of other wonderful scents in the air. Garlic and rosemary and oregano. Kate glanced at the tables, where a waiter in a white shirt and dark slacks was starting to replace the glasses and espresso cups with clean plates and silverware. The scents must have been coming from the kitchen, where they'd started preparing dinner.

Suddenly Kate's stomach grumbled loudly and she felt her face turn red.

Nick smiled. "Sounds like someone's hungry."

Starving was more like it, Kate thought.

A waiter passed with a tray loaded with hot and cold antipasti. Both Kate and Nick watched with hungry eyes.

"Know what they call that in the restaurant business?" Nick asked. "Plate envy."

"I believe it," Kate said.

Nick placed a finger on Kate's forearm. "Come on, Kate, I'm hungry too. In fact, I'm famished. What do you say we eat?"

18

KATE WAS DEFINITELY TEMPTED BY THE FOOD. BUT HOW much of that temptation was also caused by Nick himself? That was the dangerous part. She could too easily remember what had happened the last time they'd had dinner and drinks together, and how they'd wound up spending the night together in Atlantic City. And while she tried to tell herself that she had no regrets, part of her knew she most certainly did. It wasn't so much that she regretted that night. It was everything that followed that she found so hard to reconcile.

So the question was, could she trust herself to have another dinner with Nick without risking the same result?

Next to her, Nick smiled in a way that made her wonder if he could read her thoughts. "Hey, it's just dinner, okay? If I really had something else in mind, I would have tried to get you to have another drink on an empty stomach, right?"

Good point, Kate thought. "Okay, you've convinced me."

They moved to a corner table and started with an antipasto.

Nick explained that there were no menus. You ate whatever the chef felt like making that night. Kate told him about the problem with Stu and Tanner and her plan to deal with it at the Scare Fair the next night. "So . . . will you help me?" she asked.

"You mean show up at just the right moment and make sure they get the message that they're messing with the wrong people?" Nick said. "Sure, it'd be my pleasure."

Kate felt a wave of relief and gratitude sweep through her. But then she had a second thought. "You understand that I don't want them to be hurt. Just scared. You'll tell your men that, won't you?"

Nick smiled. "I don't need 'my men' for something like this. It'll just be me and Eddie."

"Eddie?"

"Eddie the Eraser."

"Why do they call him that?" Kate asked.

"'Cause when he's finished with you, there's nothing left," Nick said with a wink.

"Seriously, Nick," Kate said, not amused by the implications. "These are just a couple of high school boys who don't know what they're getting themselves into. You know I'll appreciate anything you can do, but I really, really don't want them to be hurt."

"I understand," Nick said. "Now, how about some wine, okay? Let's relax."

Kate agreed, and Nick ordered a bottle of wine. They ate the antipasto, sipped their wine, and talked—about school, college, and movies. Dinner arrived—first a small plate of pasta, then a veal dish—and it was delicious. Nick was charming and funny, and Kate was reminded of what had attracted her to him in the first place. They talked and laughed and, for a while, Kate not only forgot why they'd met to talk in the first place, but about all the other problems in her life as well. Few people had the power to captivate Kate's attention so raptly.

And then dinner was over much too quickly and just like that night in Atlantic City, Kate found herself not wanting the evening to end. Nick dabbed his lips with his napkin and gave her a look.

"What about the bill?" Kate asked, assuming the waiter would bring them one.

"There's no bill here," Nick said, and started to get up.

Kate joined him, and they stepped out into the cool late-October night. The scent of woodsmoke was in the air.

"Someone's got a fire going," Nick said.

"I love that smell," Kate said, imagining cuddling up next to the fire. But when she tried to put a face on the guy she was cuddling with, it kept flitting back and forth between Teddy and Nick. And Nick seemed to be winning.

The temptation to keep the night going was strong. Day by day it was getting more difficult to see Teddy and easier to see Nick. Just this past summer Randi had teased her, saying, "If you can't be with the one you love, love the one you're with." Now she couldn't get those words out of her head.

They walked toward his car slowly and, thanks to the wine, a bit unsteadily. Once, when they accidentally bumped shoulders, were both quick to say "Sorry" as if both needed to make sure the other knew it wasn't intentional.

Kate giggled.

"What?" Nick asked.

"I don't know," she said. "It's just funny how careful we're both trying to be."

As Nick drove her back to the high school parking lot, Kate wondered what she would have said had he decided to take her someplace else. She was glad she wouldn't have to decide.

Nick parked next to her car and got out when Kate did. That wasn't like him, and she wondered what he was doing. She decided it might be a good idea to remind him of why she'd wanted to meet him in the first place.

"Nick, really, I just want to thank you ahead of time for agreeing to help us," she said. "It really means a lot."

Nick nodded silently and opened the door to her car for her. By now, the friction between them was palpable. As Kate stepped past him to get in, it was almost hard to breathe. Part of her wanted so much for him to stop her, take her in his arms, and kiss her.

"Kate," he said.

She spun around and stepped into his arms. They kissed. And why not? What did it matter, now that her father was in jail and Nick's father was well on his way to taking over the Blessings' territory? So what if their fathers hated each other? All that was in the past. They were no longer representatives of rival organizations. This was no longer a Romeo and Juliet scenario of forbidden love while the Capulets and Montagues fought.

Nick's kisses were gentle but firm. Kate feasted on his lips while she clung to him. She was hardly aware of the cars passing on the road beside the school until someone rolled down his window and shouted, "Get a room!"

Nick eased his hold on her and gazed questioningly into her eyes.

Kate shook her head. She stepped back. They'd had a moment and she'd enjoyed every second of it, but she wasn't going to make the same mistake twice. She and Nick had a long way to go before they could get back to where they'd been that night in Atlantic City. She leaned forward and quickly kissed him one last time on the lips.

"Thank you for dinner," she said, and started to get into the car.

"Kate, wait." Nick held the door, preventing her from pulling the door closed.

She looked up at him from the driver's seat. A bright quarter moon hung over his shoulder. Nick had a pained look on his face. "What do I have to do?" he asked, as if he were at his wit's end.

"Give me time, Nick," she said.

"How much time?"

"I don't know."

"But . . . it's so obvious."

"It was obvious to me once before, Nick," Kate said. "You had a chance."

He hung his head. "I was an idiot."

She didn't think it was an act. She truly believed he was being sincere and that his regret was real. But it didn't change her mind. She'd been burned by him once. She'd be a fool to let herself be burned by him again. Next time, she'd have to be certain.

Nick let go of the door, and she started to close it. But then she stopped. "You'll be at the Scare Fair, right? You won't let me down?"

"Definitely," Nick said.

Kate changed her mind and went to school the next day. Leo's condition was slowly improving, and it occurred to Kate that if she didn't go to school again, and then showed up at the Scare Fair that night, a teacher or administrator might notice.

The Scare Fair dance was held each year on the Friday night before Halloween. It began at six p.m. for the younger kids, and then, at nine p.m. became a dance for the older kids. Kate decided to wear a yellow tracksuit with a black stripe down the sides and carry a fake sword—Uma Thurman from *Kill Bill*. When she got to the dance, half the kids hadn't even bothered to wear a costume. As usual, the most elaborate costumes—pirates, queens, ghosts—were worn by the teachers, administrators, and volunteer parent-chaperones.

As soon as Kate got there, she began looking around for Stu, Tanner, and Randi. Up on a stage, a local band called the Ambiguous Gents was playing a loud mixture of rock and hip-hop. Among those who wore masks, it wasn't easy to tell who was who. If it weren't for her substantial chest, Randi might have gone unnoticed in her red and black Lieutenant Uhura *Star Trek* outfit. Kate went over and tapped her on the shoulder.

"I thought you outgrew the Trekky thing," Kate said, speaking loudly to be heard over the music.

"Do you mean physically or mentally?" Randi asked.

"Both," said Kate.

"It's the only costume I have." Randi shrugged, then moved close to Kate and dropped her voice. "Have you seen Stu and Tanner? Are they here?"

"It's too early," Kate said. "You told them we'd meet at ten o'clock in the library, right?"

"Right, and exactly what's the plan?" Randi asked. "Considering they're expecting us to give them five thousand dollars we don't have."

"We'll give them something else instead," Kate said.

"Like what?"

"Some friends of mine."

Randi's eyes widened, and she bit her lip. "Kate, I'm really scared. If this doesn't work and they turn me in . . ."

"You mean if they turn us in," Kate corrected her.

"Right. If they turn us in, my life is ruined," Randi said. "Our lives are ruined!"

"Not quite," Kate said. "It would be a first offense for both of us on what most people would consider a victimless crime."

"What does that mean?" Randi asked.

"No jail time," said Kate.

"But I'd have a conviction on my record," Randi said. "Anyone thinking of hiring me for a job would see it. No one would give me a decent job. I'd have to spend the rest of my life flipping burgers or cleaning houses."

Kate shook her head. "Youthful offender treatment."

"What's that?" Randi asked.

"You're under eighteen, so you'd qualify," Kate said. "You get a provisional conviction. If you have a clean record for five years after that, they expunge the records. It's like you were never convicted in the first place."

"I've never heard of that," Randi said.

"Your lawyer would know," Kate said.

"Wait a minute!" Randi gasped. "My lawyer? My father's business just went bankrupt. We're practically living hand to mouth. How am I going to afford a lawyer?"

"First rule of life in an organization," Kate said. "When you've got a moneymaking scam going, always put away enough for a good criminal defense lawyer."

"No offense or anything," Randi said, "but that doesn't seem to have worked for your father."

"There's a limit to how much anyone can put away," Kate said. "Unfortunately, ten million dollars is way over it."

"I was trying to save some money until you came along and said you needed nine thousand for your guys," Randi reminded her.

"Oops. Forgot about that," Kate said with a slightly embarrassed chuckle.

"I can't believe you can find humor in this situation," Randi said. "I'm dying here thinking my whole future is on the line and you think it's a big laugh."

"I don't think it's a big laugh," Kate said. "But I also don't think we have much to worry about. Stu and Tanner are in for a seriously rude surprise."

"You hope," Randi said.

The Scare Fair dance was held in the gym, but the fair for the younger kids was held in the library, where the long stacks of books could be turned into tunnels and caves. At 9:55 p.m., Stu and Tanner arrived at the dance. Stu was wearing a clown outfit, and Tanner was dressed as Spider-Man.

Kate waved at them to meet in the middle of the dancing crowd. The guys met them. Kate noticed that both were looking around nervously, as if half expecting an ambush.

"Ready?" Stu asked.

"In the library," Kate said.

"Let's go," said Tanner.

"You guys go first," Kate said. "We'll come in a few minutes. It'll look too suspicious if all four of us go out in the hall at the same time."

Stu and Tanner slipped out through the doors at the back of the gym. Kate and Randi remained behind in the gym for a moment.

"So where are your friends?" Randi hissed.

"He said he'd be here," Kate whispered back.

"Oh, great," Randi said nervously. "That's just fabulous. He said they'd be here and they're not here. Meanwhile my entire future is hanging by a thread."

"Chill," Kate said.

"Easy for you to say," Randi said.

"Hey, my future's on a thread too," Kate said.

"But that's nothing new for you," Randi said. "For me, this is a whole new level of stress and anxiety, and I'm too young to start taking Xanax."

"We can stall," Kate said.

Randi checked her watch. "We're supposed to meet the boys in the library right now. They know we're here. If we're late, they're going to suspect something."

She was right. Kate had no idea how to stall in this situation. "We'd better go to the library."

"And then what?" Randi whispered as they started out of the gym. "They say, 'Where's the five thousand?' And we say . . . ?"

"Chill, Randi," Kate said. "I mean it."

They walked down the hall in their costumes. Ahead of them, the library was lit and open, but empty. The entrance had been decorated to resemble a cave, and inside were scarecrows and witches and spiders and other things to entertain the younger kids.

Kate and Randi went in and walked down a long row of books toward the back of the library. When they go there, they found they were alone.

"Where are they?" Randi whispered, looking around.

"I don't know," Kate said, although she had a feeling she knew why the boys weren't in sight.

"You think they know?" Randi asked.

Kate brought her finger to her lips, but it was too late.

"Think we know what?" a voice from behind them said. Kate and Randi spun around. Stu and Tanner (clown and Spider-Man) came out from behind a row of books.

Randi was speechless. She started to look around with a panicked expression on her face.

"What're you looking for?" Stu asked.

"Oh, nothing," Randi gasped, her eyes still darting about. Kate knew her friend had warned her that she wasn't cool in a situation like this, but Kate had never realized quite how uncool that could be.

"Wait a minute," Tanner said. "She's looking for someone. This is a setup."

19

NOW STU AND TANNER STARTED TO LOOK AROUND.
Kate knew that if they got spooked and left before Nick
got there, the whole plan would be blown. She tried to
think of what she could say to get them to stay. "It's not a setup. I
don't know what you're talking about."

Tanner/Spider-Man gave her a rueful look. "Give me a break,
Kate." He turned to Randi. "Where's the money?"

Randi gave Kate a desperate look.

"You don't have it, do you?" Tanner said.

Randi stared at the floor and shook her head.

Tanner smirked. "Have fun explaining your phony driver's
license scam to the cops." He turned to Stu. "Come on, let's get
out of here."

The boys started out of the library. Kate wanted to kick herself
for believing that Nick would come to their aid.

"They're really going to tell the cops!" Randy gasped in a
hoarse whisper. "Oh, my god! This is the end! I'm going to jail.

And you're going too, Kate. Don't say I didn't warn you. I told you from the start that if they got me, I'd give you up in a heartbeat. I love you like a sister, but I'm not going alone."

Kate believed her. And where the hell was Nick? He'd promised to be there. Kate dug out her cell phone and speed-dialed him.

"Kate?" Nick answered.

"Where are you?"

"On our way," Nick said, then added with a chuckle. "We got lost. Guess it's been a while since we've been to school."

"Not funny," Kate said. "The guys figured out it was a setup and ran. They could be on their way to the cops right now."

"Crap," Nick said. "Look, we're just pulling into the parking lot now. What do these guys look like?"

"Spider-Man and a clown," Kate said.

"What?"

"They're in costume," Kate said. "Remember, it's Halloween."

"Okay, hang on, we're in the parking lot," Nick said. "Okay, yeah, I think I see them. One of them drive a Jeep Grand Cherokee?"

"Yes," said Kate.

The next thing Kate heard were car tires screeching and Nick yelling, "Eddie, over there!" Then there were slapping footsteps and heavy breathing.

Suddenly Kate had a foreboding feeling. "Nick?" she said into the phone. "Nick?"

The cell phone had gone dead. Kate snapped it shut. "Come on!" she said to Randi, and hurried out of the library.

"What's wrong?" Randi asked as she ran after her.

"My friend's out there and he's going to get Tanner and Stu," Kate said.

"What's wrong with that?" Randi asked, puffing as she ran to keep up. "I thought that's what you wanted."

"Yes and no," Kate said as she raced down the hallway. "I want to scare them and make sure they learn a lesson. But my friend may have other ideas."

"Who exactly is your friend?" Randi asked.

"Nick," Kate said. "Remember, from the boat show?"

"I thought you were going to get a couple of your thugs," Randi said.

"What do you think Nick is?" Kate gasped as she ran.

"He didn't look like a thug to me," Randi panted.

"It's more like he's in charge of thugs," Kate said.

They hurried outside and into the dark. The high school parking lot was filled with cars. The sky was covered with dark clouds, blocking the moon and starlight.

"See anything?" Kate asked.

Randi shook her head.

Breathing hard from the run, Kate started to walk quickly among the cars.

"Where are you going?" Randi asked.

"They have to be around here somewhere," Kate said.

Down at the end of a row of cars, a silver Mercedes with oversize rims was parked on a diagonal across two parking spots. Kate placed her hand on the hood. It felt hot. She was sure it was

Nick's car. Nearby was Tanner's Jeep Cherokee with the driver's side door open and the headlights on. But there was no sign of the guys. Kate imagined what could have happened. Tanner and Stu were probably just getting into the Jeep when Nick and his friend Eddie had arrived.

And that meant either Nick and Eddie had grabbed Tanner and Stu before they got into the Jeep, or the boys had tried to run. Once again, Kate looked around. So where were they?

"Ooof!" A loud grunt came from behind a boxy yellow rented truck in the corner of the parking lot. Kate hurried toward it.

She found them on the other side of the truck. Nick and a bigger man had backed Tanner and Stu against the truck. Stu, in his clown suit, was lying on the ground, doubled over with his arms wrapped across his stomach as if he'd just had the wind knocked out of him by a punch to the stomach. The bigger man, wearing baggy jeans and an oversize football jersey, stood over Stu as if waiting to see if he could get back to his feet.

Tanner was backed against the truck. Nick was holding him there with one hand against his shoulder. Tanner's Spider-Man mask was off, and he was holding his hands against his face. Blood was seeping out from between his fingers as he gave Kate a miserable look. Now she noticed that one of his eyes was swollen and the front of the Spider-Man costume had a dark, wet stain.

"I told you I didn't want you to hurt them," Kate said angrily.

"Oh hi, Kate," Nick said, almost as if it was a surprise that she was there. "Eddie, this is my friend Kate."

"Hey, Eddie," Kate said.

The big guy wearing baggy jeans and the oversize football jersey turned and grinned at her, revealing a gold tooth. "Hi."

On the ground, Stu groaned. Tanner tried to slide down the truck as if to get away, but Nick grabbed him by the shoulder and dragged him back.

Randi joined them, breathing hard.

"This is my friend Randi," Kate said. "You met her at the boat show, remember?"

"Nice to see you again," Nick said.

"Same here," said Randi.

"These are the guys, right?" Nick said. "We didn't get the wrong ones, did we?"

"These are the right ones," Kate said. "But why did you have to hurt them?"

"This is nothing," Nick said. "Just a love tap."

With another groan, Stu managed to get to his hands and knees. Eddie took a step toward him as if to kick him in the ribs.

"Hold on," Kate said. "Eddie, wait a minute." She turned and looked at Tanner. "I told these guys not to hurt you. Obviously they're not real good at following directions, but I'll try again. Anything you'd like to say?"

"Just call these guys off," Tanner said, his voice slightly muffled by the hand he was holding against his nose.

"I will, as long as you promise not to cause any more trouble," Kate said.

"No more trouble," Stu groaned, still on his knees on the ground. "I promise."

"Hey," Eddie the Eraser said, "know how we're always talking about kicking the crap out of some clown? This time, it's true!"

"You're a funny guy, Eddie," Nick said, and turned to Kate. "What are the names of these two tough guys?"

"Spider-Man with a bloody nose is Tanner Westfall," Kate said. "And the clown on the ground is Stu McLean."

"So later on tonight you'll give me their phone numbers and addresses," Nick said to Kate. "That way we'll know how to find them again if we need to."

"You won't need to," Tanner said.

"That's what I'd like to think," Nick said. "But you never know. Some guys just aren't that smart."

"I think these two will be," Kate said. "And I really appreciate your help with this."

"No problem, Kate," Nick said. "Call me later with those addresses and phone numbers, okay?"

"Definitely," Kate said.

Nick turned to Tanner and Stu. "So listen, Spider-Man and trusty clown sidekick, like I said before, this was nothing. Just a love tap, understand? I have to deal with you two again, you'll be lucky if you can get around on crutches. Understand?"

Stu and Tanner nodded.

"Okay, Eddie, let's go." Nick and Eddie the Eraser walked away in the dark, leaving Kate, Randi, and the boys. Tanner was still leaning against the truck. Stu slowly got to his feet and brushed the dirt off his hands. His clown mask was at an angle and his costume was smudged with dirt.

"You guys okay?" Kate asked.

"Just great," Tanner grumbled, his hands still covering his face.

"How's your nose?" Randi asked.

"Probably broken," Tanner said. "And what's this act pretending like you suddenly care?"

"I do care," Kate said. "I don't like to see anyone get hurt."

"Then why did you send those goons after us?" groaned Stu.

"Are you serious?" Randi said. "You threatened to turn us in to the cops."

"That was supposed to be just between us," Tanner grunted. "Why'd you have to bring in the mob?"

"You must be joking," Kate said. "You were blackmailing Randi. You wanted five thousand dollars. You were threatening to ruin her life. Maybe you don't understand how serious that is."

"We do now," Stu muttered.

"So seriously," Kate said, "I want to make you an offer."

"One we can't refuse?" Tanner asked archly.

"One you shouldn't refuse," Kate said. "You guys made a nasty video of Randi and put it on the Internet. So she did the same to you. And then you threatened to blackmail her and, no offense or anything, you got what you deserved. Personally, I think this is a really good time to declare a truce."

Tanner and Stu glanced at each other.

"No tricks," Kate cautioned them. "I mean it. You heard what my friends said. If I have to call them again, I won't be responsible for the damage they do."

Stu and Tanner agreed. Kate would have preferred shaking hands, but Tanner's were bloody and Stu's were dirty. Still, she had a feeling the boys would honor the agreement.

The boys left in Tanner's Jeep, and Kate and Randi walked back to their cars.

"I don't think I can deal with this anymore," Randi said. "I mean, the money's been great, but it's not worth the ulcer I'll probably wake up with tomorrow morning. You won't be angry, will you? I mean, if I back out of this?"

Kate shook her head. "I think you're right. We had a good run, but too many people know about it now. Can you and Shane erase everything on the computer and get rid of the printer and laminator?"

"No prob. I've become an expert at destroying files. And eBay's the best when it comes to disposing incriminating equipment."

"Great," Kate said. They'd reached her car.

"So, I thought you weren't going to see Nick anymore," Randi said.

"There's a difference between seeing him and needing his help," Kate said.

"Why do I think you could have asked someone else for help if you'd wanted to?" Randi asked.

Kate felt emotions begin to creep up on her. Her feelings were like strangers hiding in the dark and waiting to jump out at unexpected moments. She'd be going along fine, thinking she had everything under control, and then, *bang*! Everything would go bonkers. Tears began to blur her vision.

"What about Teddy?" Randi asked.

"Good question," Kate said with a sniff. "His parents are totally freaked out about my father. They're making it almost impossible for us to see each other."

"And the problem with Nick is that your fathers are mortal enemies?" Randi asked.

"It may not matter anymore," Kate said, dabbing her eyes. "The two organizations have sort of merged. Our fathers may hate each other, but otherwise it's just supposed to be one big happy family."

"Then what's stopping you from getting together now?" Randi asked.

"I told you," Kate said. "I don't trust him."

"Oh, great," Randi said sarcastically. "So you can't see the guy you can trust, and you can't trust the guy you can see."

Kate nodded, once again admiring her friend's gift for summation. She dabbed the tears out of her eyes.

Randi gave her a hug. "I owe you a big thanks. Not just for saving my butt tonight, but for showing me that I'm just not cut out for this kind of stuff. From now on, no more scams and ventures. I'm back on the straight and narrow."

"What about your car and nice clothes?" Kate asked.

Randi shrugged. "It was fun while it lasted. Somehow I managed to live a long time without that stuff. I'm not saying I don't want it anymore. I'm just saying that from now on, I plan to live on what I can afford through legitimate means."

It may have sounded like a statement, but Kate realized her friend was asking her a question: Could she live that way too?

20

LATER, KATE CALLED NICK, AS PROMISED, AND GAVE HIM the names and addresses for Stu and Tanner.

"I really don't think you'll need this," she said. "I can't imagine those two bothering us again."

"I'd tend to think you're right," Nick said. "But you never know."

"You really saved our skins," Kate said. "How can I thank you?"

"You could start by telling me why they were trying to blackmail you," Nick said.

Now that she and Randi had decided to abandon the phony driver's license scheme, Kate didn't mind telling Nick about it.

"Sounds like a nice little scam," Nick said. "You made some good money?"

"For a while," Kate said. "But it definitely feels like it's time to get out."

"So what do you think you'll do next?" Nick asked.

"I have absolutely no idea," Kate said.

"Maybe we can get together and talk about it," Nick said.

Kate understood what he was saying, and she was dismayed by the keen temptation she felt. A slight flicker of hesitation distracted her, but only for a moment. "Why do I think that, if I ask how, when, and where, you'll suggest we do it over drinks?"

"Maybe because that's secretly what you want," said Nick.

She knew he was right. That *was* what she secretly wanted. Not just to have a drink, but to look into those deep, intense eyes and feel his arms around her and his lips on hers.

Almost immediately, Kate felt guilty. What about Teddy? What about being honest and faithful? Even though they'd just spoken two days before, Kate suddenly felt the need to hear his voice. What excuse could she give him for insisting they speak again so soon? Their last conversation had been cut short. Thanksgiving vacation was coming. She assumed Teddy would be coming home, but the last time they'd spoken, he hadn't said anything about it. That sounded like a good enough reason to speak to him. Maybe they could arrange a secret meeting.

She IM'd him, asking if they could talk by phone.

He IM'd back a phone number, but when Kate called it, she got a message: "Hi, it's Carter. Leave a message."

Kate hung up. He'd given her gorgeous blond Carter's phone number. At first it rattled her, but then she thought, *Wait a minute. If anything was going on between them, he wouldn't have given her that number, right?*

Kate was just about to call back when her phone rang. It was Carter's number.

"Blessing?" Teddy said when she answered.

"Teddy, I'm sorry to bother you," Kate said.

"You're not bothering me, Blessing," Teddy said. "Happy Halloween. Doing anything fun?"

"Randi and I went to the dance," Kate replied, hoping the lie of omission wasn't as bad as a lie of commission. "You?"

"They're having a Scary Movie marathon," Teddy said, "but one can take just so much."

Kate pictured the auditorium where the movies were probably being shown, and grimaced slightly as she recalled what had happened the night she'd sat there with Teddy. *All those eyes staring at me . . .*

"So how are you?" Teddy's question brought her back from the painful memory.

"I miss you." The answer was out of her lips before her brain had time to think about it.

Teddy dropped his voice. "I miss you, too."

Kate was glad to hear him say it, but wondered why he felt the need to drop his voice. "Where are you?" she asked.

"Hanging around the student center," Teddy replied. "We're taking a break from the movies."

Kate listened more closely and heard voices in the background. If he was on Carter's phone, then it made sense that she was nearby. It also might explain why Teddy had lowered his voice. Kate felt her spirits drop.

"Blessing?" Teddy said. "Still there?"

"Yes." Kate told herself to get a grip. It was easy to allow doubts and suspicions to fill the empty places, but before she got too wound up, it was important to remember that she hadn't exactly been sitting around doing nothing in his absence. Not with Nick around. If anyone should be suspicious of anyone, Teddy probably should have been suspicious of her.

"So what's up?" Teddy asked.

"I was wondering about Thanksgiving," Kate said.

"It's a national holiday for giving thanks, always celebrated on the fourth Thursday of November," Teddy said. "Strangely, the Canadians celebrate it on the second Monday of October, but you know, things are different up there."

Kate felt a smile grow on her face. "That's not what I meant."

"I know," Teddy said. "But aren't you impressed with the incredibly useful and important knowledge they're filling my head with up here?"

The smile grew broader. She remembered how good he was at making her relax and laugh.

"So the real answer isn't good, Blessing," Teddy said. "My parents are one step ahead of us. Suddenly, this year, the Fitzgeralds Thanksgiving's going to be celebrated in Palm Springs."

"Oh." Kate felt her heart sink. She wasn't sure what depressed her more, the fact that she couldn't see him or the fact that he seemed so passive about it.

"I'm sorry, Blessing," Teddy said. "My parents are all over

this. I've never seen them like this before. They're doing everything they possibly can to make sure we can't see each other."

"There's no way?" Kate said.

"I wish, Blessing, really. But my parents haven't let up. I know they're checking on me all the time to make sure they know where I am. If I thought there was a chance I could see you without them knowing, I would."

She believed him. And yet she wished he would sound more angry or upset or anything that would make her feel like he still cared. It would have been so much sweeter if he'd acted like he really wanted to see her no matter what his parents said, and then she could say no, it was too risky.

In the background she heard a girl laugh. Was it Carter?

"So . . . I guess that means I won't be seeing you over Christmas, either?" Kate asked.

"It won't last forever," Teddy said. "It can't. At some point, they'll calm down."

"And in the meantime, all we can do is wait?" Kate asked, feeling herself grow upset.

Teddy didn't answer.

"And then what about next year?" Kate asked. "You'll be at Stanford, and I'll . . . I don't even know where I'll be."

"Then maybe I won't go to Stanford," Teddy said.

"But that's where you've applied, isn't it? Early admission?"

"Yes."

"And nowhere else," Kate said.

"Only because those are the rules of early admission," Teddy replied. "Blessing, please, don't get upset."

That was so Teddy, so stiff upper lip and all that civilized baloney. But how could he *not* be upset? Didn't he feel like a marionette tied to strings controlled by his parents? What about all those speeches he'd given her about how he could do what he wanted because ultimately his parents needed him more than he needed them?

Kate was tempted to remind him of that, but knew it would only make him more defensive and possibly even angry. And what was the point of doing that? But she had to say something. "Teddy, seriously, doesn't it bother you?"

"Of course it bothers me," Teddy said.

Then why don't you act like it does? Kate wondered.

And, as if he could read her thoughts, he added, "I guess I just believe it'll work out, Blessing. It's the eternal optimist in me."

Either that or it's the gorgeous blonde sitting nearby, Kate thought.

21

LEO LEFT THE HOSPITAL, AND DARLENE HAD EVERYONE over to her house for Thanksgiving dinner to celebrate. Only these days, "everyone" meant Kate and her mother and brother.

"What about Joey Buttons and some of the other guys from the crew?" Kate asked in the kitchen, where she and her mom were helping Darlene with the turkey. Leo and Sonny Jr. were in the living room watching football.

"Not since they joined the Blattarias," Darlene said. "Leo won't have nothing to do with them. Says they're all traitors."

Amanda turned to Kate. "He always was your father's most loyal man."

It still irked Kate to hear her mother talk about loyalty, but then, she had to remind herself that her father had been unfaithful for years before her mother had been.

The kitchen door swung open, and Sonny Jr. came in. That long-awaited growth spurt had finally arrived. Kate's little brother had not only shot up in height, but his shoulders had broadened as well. His hair was tastefully spiked, and he had dark stubble on his jaw. He looked more like his father than ever, and undeniably handsome.

"How's dinner coming?" he asked, plucking a roll from a basket and taking a bite from it.

"Soon," Darlene answered. "Hungry?"

"He's always hungry," Amanda said. "I fill the refrigerator one day, the next day it's empty."

"Hey, I'm a growing boy," Kate's brother said, chewing. He turned and looked at Kate. "What are you staring at?"

"I don't think you can call yourself a boy anymore," Kate said.

Sonny Jr. blinked as if he didn't understand, and then smiled when he did.

"The girls at school must be all over you like flies on honey," Darlene said.

Kate's brother blushed and turned back toward the living room.

"Hey." Amanda picked up a serving dish filled with sweet potatoes. "Don't go out empty-handed."

Sonny Jr. took the dish and left.

"Someone's going to have to keep an eye on that one," Darlene said. "And make sure he doesn't get himself into trouble."

Amanda sighed loudly. "If he's got his father's genes, there'll be nothing anyone can do."

Kate gave her mother a long look.

"What's that look about?" Amanda finally asked.

"You know," Kate said.

Amanda turned to Darlene. The two women were best friends and Kate had no doubt that Darlene knew everything about Marvin the dentist.

"What do you expect?" Darlene said to Amanda. "She's daddy's little girl. He can do no wrong."

"And I can do no right," Amanda said a bit bitterly.

"Forget it, Mom," Kate said.

"Well, you might be interested to know that Marvin's no longer in the picture," her mother said.

"What happened?" Kate asked.

"He wants to get married. He wants a wife who'll get up in the morning and make him breakfast and be waiting for him at the door when he gets home at night." Amanda glanced at Darlene, who had been precisely that kind of wife for the past forty years. "Sorry, but you know what I mean."

"That's not you," Kate said.

"That is *so* not me," Amanda agreed.

"So now what?" Kate asked.

"I don't know," her mother said. "The lease on the apartment runs out in a few days. I'm not sure it makes sense to keep it anymore."

Kate felt an involuntary thrill. "Does that mean you're coming home?"

"No place else to go," Amanda said.

Kate tried to keep from smiling.

The turkey came out of the oven, and Darlene called Leo and

Sonny Jr. in from the living room. Leo came in wearing black slacks and a black shirt. In a strange way, Kate had finally gotten what she'd wanted for him. He'd lost weight (because of the heart attack) and changed out of the old stained beige tracksuit (because it no longer fit).

"I'm glad we can be together today," he said, once everyone was seated. "For a while it looked like it was just gonna be the mothers and children. So I guess we got something to be thankful for, because at least one old guy is here."

Everyone nodded, but no one looked particularly cheerful and Kate knew why. Unless a miracle occurred, it would be a very, very long time before the other "old guy," her father Sonny, would be able to join them.

They started to eat. Darlene fixed a plate for her husband with skinless white meat, a potato, and string beans. Leo scowled. "That's it?"

"You know what the doctor said," Darlene said. "You gotta eat healthy from now on."

"But it's Thanksgiving," Leo argued.

"No exceptions," Darlene said.

Leo made a sour face. "Maybe I shouldn't have bothered. They shoulda left me on the operating table."

"Leo, that's a terrible thing to say," said Amanda.

"You think so?" Leo asked. "What do I got to live for? The organization's gone, my friends are gone. The only thing I enjoy anymore is a good meal, and now I'm not even allowed to have that."

The others shot furtive glances around the table.

"Tell you what, Darl, I promise I'll be good from now till Christmas," Leo said. "What do you say?"

Everyone knew that while Leo meant it, it was a promise he could never keep. Just like he could never stop eating sweets. Still, it was Thanksgiving.

Darlene smiled sadly and nodded, and they all watched as Leo reached for the dark meat and slathered his potato with butter. They tried to have a cheerful meal, but there wasn't a whole lot to be cheerful about. Even Kate's mom coming home was little more than a silver lining in a pretty dark cloud.

That weekend she saw Nick for another date, and once again they had a great time. But she couldn't get Teddy out of her mind. She'd never been to Palm Springs, but she'd seen enough photos to know that it was gorgeous and green, in the middle of the dessert and surrounded by mountains. It was starting to seem like there would always be mountains and vast distances between them.

After a nightcap they sat in Nick's car and kissed passionately. Nick clearly wanted the evening to continue, but Kate finally pushed his hands away. She was incredibly tempted, but that alone was reason enough to call a halt to it. If she was going to make a decision about it, she didn't want to make it in the heat of the moment. She wanted to make it when she could think rationally.

"Are you sure?" Nick asked in the car.

No, she wasn't sure at all. If only he knew how unsure she was. But she pretended she was sure, half hoping Nick would try one of those "I'm a man and I have needs" speeches that Tanner had specialized in. It hadn't worked for Tanner, but she wasn't so sure it wouldn't work with Nick.

"Why?"

"You know why," Kate said.

"Yeah, I know," Nick said ruefully. "You can't trust me. Well, doesn't it work both ways? How do I know I can trust you?"

Kate smiled. "You don't."

Nick couldn't help but grin. "Guess you got me there."

She could tell he was afraid that if he argued too much, it would turn her off. Little did he know that if he'd argued enough, he probably could have gotten what he wanted.

He dropped her off at the high school, and she drove her own car home. Her mom and Sonny Jr. had moved back into the house and Kate didn't want Amanda to know who she was seeing. As far as Amanda was concerned, Kate had gone to the movies with Randi.

When she got home, the house was brightly lit. That was strange, considering how late it was. She let herself in the front door and stood in the black marble foyer. The house was silent. "Mom?" she called. "Sonny Junior?"

No one answered. Kate felt a chill. Something wasn't right.

She glanced around, and noticed a pink Post-it stuck to the side table near the door. Kate read it:

We're at Darlene's. Leo died.

22

LEO HAD MANAGED TO LIVE FOR THREE WEEKS AFTER the first heart attack, but the second one did him in. The doctor said it had nothing to do with Thanksgiving dinner. These things just happened, he said, without rhyme or reason. But no matter what the doctor said, Kate felt devastated. Leo had been like a second father to her.

The wake would go until Thursday. The funeral would be Friday. Since Kate had already missed a lot of school, and would miss Friday, she decided to go. Going to school would help get her mind off Leo. Besides, on Thursday after school they had an FBLA event at Middletown High, in what used to be the heart of Blattaria territory, before the Blattarias took over everything in sight.

That Thursday the FBLA event in Middletown was over by 5:30. Kate thought it went well, but somehow she just wasn't as into it as she used to be. It might have been the shadow Leo's death cast over everything, or maybe the fact that senior year was almost half over, or the uncertainty about where, or even if, she'd be going to college next year. Whatever it was, Kate had a feeling a part of her life was coming to an end, and it would never be the same again.

It was dark and chilly in the parking lot outside Middletown High. Kate was surprised to see a slight sheen of white frost on the roof of her Mercedes. It was a short drive to the highway, and as Kate drove she passed gas stations and convenience stores and the sort of sleazy motel that advertised free Internet access in all rooms and special day rates. As Kate passed, she happened to glance into the parking lot. And there, among the pickup trucks and SUVs, was a familiar-looking silver Mercedes with oversize rims.

Kate's first impulse was to assume that it was someone else's car. After all, there were plenty of Silver Mercedes on the road and at least a few of them had to have oversize rims, didn't they? But suppose . . . just suppose . . . it was Nick's. What was it doing parked outside that motel?

Business? That was possible. Only Kate didn't feel good about the kinds of business it could be. Still, she kept driving toward the highway. Whatever Nick was doing was his business. It wasn't her style to spy on people. Even if, at times, it seemed like it was the style of the entire rest of the world.

The highway entrance was coming up on the right. Kate . . . passed it. At the next intersection she made a U-turn and drove back toward the motel, parking in front of a liquor store across the street. The silver Mercedes was still parked in the motel lot. Kate told herself she would wait ten minutes.

Ten minutes became fifteen, and then twenty.

Then half an hour. And then . . . well, she'd waited this long, so what harm could there be in waiting a little longer?

She waited nearly an hour. On the second floor of the motel a door opened and a man and a woman came out. Kate knew immediately that it was Nick. It wasn't until they started down the outdoor stairs and passed under the light that she became certain the woman was Tiff.

Kate couldn't believe it. It wasn't so much that she couldn't believe that Nick had lied, as the boldness of the lies. "It was over," he'd said. "It was a mistake," he'd sworn.

Kate slid down in the seat of her car, praying Nick wouldn't notice it was parked across the street. She peeked up just enough to watch Nick walk Tiff to a dark sedan and give her a quick kiss, then walk back across the parking lot toward the silver Mercedes. A moment later, headlights bright, the dark sedan pulled out of the parking lot, followed by the Mercedes. Both cars started down the road away from the motel.

Kate's stomach turned into an angry knot. Thank God she hadn't trusted him. Thank God she'd kept her head the previous weekend. Her shoulders tightened, and she began to feel a headache creep up the back of her neck. What she'd just seen was truly unbelievable.

That's it, Kate told herself. *That's the end of Nick Blattaria. Now and forever, once and for all.*

But it wasn't. A block away, Tiff's car went through an intersection. Nick's car got to the intersection and suddenly made a U-turn.

He was coming back.

Kate caught her breath with sudden surprise and nervousness. But it quickly passed. So what if he'd seen her? So what if he was coming back to ask if she was spying on him. At this point, what did it really matter?

A few moments later, the Mercedes pulled up next to her and the window went down. "Surprise, surprise," Nick said.

Kate forced a smile onto her face. "Hello, Nick."

"Mind if I ask what you're doing here?" Nick asked.

"I was driving back from an FBLA meeting at the high school and I noticed your car in the motel parking lot."

Nick nodded. "I actually believe you. You're not the stalker type."

"Thank you," Kate said.

Nick looked around. "Mind if I join you?"

"I can't imagine why," Kate said.

"Maybe just to say good-bye," Nick said.

It hurt to hear him say that. And yet she knew that that was the way it had to be. "All right."

He pulled his car in front of hers and parked. She reached over and opened her passenger door for him.

He sat down and stared straight ahead, not saying anything.

"It's not like you to be so quiet," Kate said.

Nick hung his head and stared at the floor of the car. "It was a one-time thing, Kate. For old times' sake."

"You don't expect me to believe that, do you?" Kate asked.

A bittersweet smile crossed Nick's lips.

"You think it's funny?" Kate asked.

"Here's what's funny," Nick said. "I'm telling you the truth. But for once, I can't blame you for not believing me."

"Actions speak louder than words," Kate said.

Nick nodded. "Yeah, so I've heard." He bent forward, resting his elbows on his knees and clasping his hands together. "I blew it, Kate. There's no one to blame but me. I'm sorry. If I were you, I'd never be able to trust me either."

For once, Kate believed him. Maybe it was the body language more than the words. She felt a heavy sadness and regret, but he was right. This time, it didn't matter. Fool me once, shame on you. Fool me twice, shame on me. Fool me three times? Only she knew she hadn't really been fooled the second time. She'd come close, but had stepped back in the nick of time.

Kate turned and faced him, offering him her hand.

Nick looked up surprised.

"You said you wanted to say good-bye," Kate said.

"Yeah." He shook her hand.

"Have a good life, Nick," Kate said.

Nick reached for the door handle, then stopped and looked back at her. "You know, we've still got business to discuss."

"It'll wait," Kate said. "Good-bye, Nick."

23

SHE'D CRIED ON THE WAY HOME. MAYBE MORE FOR herself than for Nick. It just didn't seem fair that it had to be this way. Why couldn't Nick change? Why couldn't she change him? But maybe that was something she could understand from her parents' marriage. Her father was the way he was and wouldn't, or couldn't, change. Again, maybe her mother was right. Slow and steady was better than fast and furious.

Only, without Nick or Teddy, she had neither.

She got home and keyed in the code to open the driveway gate. As she drove up the driveway, she noticed a dark green car parked in the circle. It looked familiar, but for a moment she couldn't place it. Then she could.

It was Teddy's car.

Kate didn't understand. What in the world was he doing there? What about his parents? What about school?

She let herself into the house. Voices were coming from the kitchen. Kate hurried toward them. When she got there, Teddy was sitting at the kitchen counter with Sonny Jr. and her mother. Kate stopped and stared at him.

"Uh, excuse me," Teddy said, rising from his seat. "I think Kate and I have some things to talk about."

"But you'll stay for dinner?" Kate's mom asked eagerly.

"I'd love to, thanks," Teddy said. He turned to Kate. "Sorry to surprise you like this."

"No, it's . . . okay," Kate stammered. "I'm just . . . stunned."

Teddy nodded as if he understood. "Is there someplace we can go talk?"

Kate took him into the living room and closed the double-glass doors. They sat down on the black leather couch. Kate had a thousand questions, but she decided to wait and hear what Teddy had to say first.

"Private boarding schools have different schedules from other schools," he began. "More like college. Our Christmas vacation starts on Saturday."

"But today's Thursday," Kate said.

"I got a call early this morning from my mother," Teddy said. "She said my father was going to be indicted this morning for insider trading."

Kate stared at him, not comprehending.

"That's why he was so freaked out about the wiretaps," Teddy explained. "It was completely accidental. The FBI got evidence and information they weren't even looking for. They handed it over to the Securities and Exchange Commission, and that resulted in the indictment."

Kate thought she was beginning to understand. "So . . . if the FBI hadn't been investigating my father, they never would have caught *your* father?"

Teddy smiled slightly and nodded. "Kind of ironic, don't you think?"

"Oh, Teddy, I'm so sorry," Kate said.

Teddy shook his head. "Don't apologize. It's not your fault. My father was breaking the law. He was doing something both illegal and unfair. I don't want to say he deserved it, but I'm incredibly disappointed in him. That's the difference between our fathers. Your father never pretended he was something else. My father did. He pretended to be the great, upstanding citizen when he was really breaking the law."

Teddy was too polite to add, "Just like yours," but Kate understood regardless.

"So what does this mean?" she asked.

Once again, Teddy relaxed and smiled. "It means that I'm not going away over Christmas. I can be here with you. It means that while I'll probably go back to school when Christmas is over, I can come home and see you every weekend if I want."

"What about your mom?" Kate asked.

"Doesn't matter." He took her hand in his. "From now on, we can be together, Kate. As much as we want."

Kate forced a smile onto her face. It was all too much

happening too fast. She didn't know what to think. She didn't know how to feel. Was this what she really wanted?

The next morning, Friday, Kate awoke early to the sound of rain pouring down outside. Still half asleep, her first thought was that it was okay, she didn't have to go anywhere. She could stay in bed, maybe even sleep a little longer. But then she remembered what day it was. Leo's funeral.

Kate closed her eyes and let her head sink back into the pillow. *Oh, Leo*, she thought sadly. *I miss you already, and it hasn't even been a week since you died.*

"Everyone, up!" her mother called from downstairs. After all those months with her gone, it was strangely reassuring to hear her yelling again. "Come on, we got a funeral to go to."

Kate dragged herself out of bed. She wasn't looking forward to this day. Teddy, always the sweetheart, had offered to go with her, but she'd declined. Not just because he didn't know Leo or Darlene, but because she still needed time to sort out her feelings.

They rode in the limo. Outside, the cold rain streaked the car's windows and splashed down onto the dreary, gray December landscape.

"Why does it always seem to rain at funerals?" Amanda asked with a shiver. She was wearing a black dress and coat. Sonny Jr. was also dressed in black, with a white shirt and black tie. Kate wore a dark blue pantsuit.

The limo turned through tall black gates and into the cemetery.

The grass was a dull greenish gray. Rain drops dripped from the bare gray branches of the trees. The sky was slate-colored.

The limo stopped near the grave site, a dark rectangular hole in the ground. A green tarp next to it hid the dirt that would be shoveled back over the casket later. A dozen yards away, a yellow backhoe was parked behind a tree and two men in dark green ponchos leaned on shovels and smoked cigarettes.

Holding their coats closed, Kate and her mother and brother got out of the limo. The driver handed them black umbrellas. Sonny held his over Amanda as they walked toward the grave site and stood while other cars stopped and more people got out. Uncle Benny Hacksaw, Joey Buttons, and the other guys from the organization were there. Even though they'd joined the Blattarias, Kate didn't mind. This wasn't about gang rivalries. It was about paying respect to someone they all liked and admired.

They huddled around the open grave while the priest said a prayer. Women sobbed, and men looked grim. At one point Kate was vaguely aware of movement behind her, as if someone was making his way through the crowd.

"Am I late?" a voice whispered.

Kate recognized it immediately and spun around.

"Dad!" Sonny Jr. gasped.

The priest stopped. Heads turned. Murmurs broke out in the crowd. Sonny was wearing black slacks and a turtleneck and a black cloth overcoat that was about two sizes too large for him.

Sonny grinned and pressed his fingers to his lips. "Not so loud."

First Kate hugged him, and then Sonny Jr. Amanda gave him a bittersweet smile and kissed him on the cheek.

The crowd was still murmuring. Everyone was staring at Sonny. The priest cleared his throat loudly and continued the prayer.

"How'd you get out?" Kate whispered.

"I didn't," Sonny whispered back, and jerked his head. Kate looked around and saw the green unmarked police cars parked at the curb and the men in gray raincoats scattered around the perimeter of the crowd.

"I don't get it," said Sonny Jr.

"I'll explain later," Sonny said.

The funeral ended, but the rain didn't. By now, everyone was cold and wet and eager to get into their cars. Sonny walked with his family toward the limo. The men in gray raincoats moved toward them, as if to make sure Sonny didn't suddenly try to make a run for it.

Sonny stopped a dozen feet from the limo.

"You can't come with us?" Sonny Jr. asked, disappointed.

Sonny shook his head. "It's going to be a while before I can go anywhere."

"What happened?" Amanda asked as the rain continued to fall around them.

"I made a deal," Sonny whispered. "Now that Leo's gone, it's not gonna matter."

"A deal?" Kate's mom repeated. "You mean, witness protection?"

"We're not going to have to change our names and move away, are we?" Sonny Jr. asked.

"Maybe not," Sonny said. "If the cops take the Blattaria organization down, there's not going to be anyone looking for revenge because they'll all be behind bars."

Then I won't have to leave Teddy, Kate thought.

The rain grew harder and became a dull roar. Even with the umbrellas, they were all getting soaked.

"You guys better get into the limo," Sonny said. "Come visit me soon and I'll tell you the rest, okay?"

Kate and Sonny Jr. both hugged their father and promised they'd come as soon as they could. Sonny turned his gaze on his wife.

"You kids go get in the limo," Amanda said. "I want to talk to your father for a moment."

Kate and Sonny Jr. did as they were told, but once inside the limo, they watched through the windows. It was difficult to read the expressions on their faces, but the conversation ended with Amanda kissing her husband on the cheek.

Inside the limo, Sonny Jr. whispered. "That can't be a bad sign."

Outside, Amanda came hurriedly toward the limo and the men in the gray raincoats walked toward Sonny. Suddenly Kate had a thought and rolled down the window. "Dad?"

Sonny turned.

"When are they going to take down the Blattarias?" Kate asked.

"They're doing it right now," her father answered. "Otherwise, it wouldn't have been safe for me to come."

A little while later, Kate parked on a street in Flyndale. Her mother couldn't understand why she didn't go back to Darlene's for the big dinner after the funeral, but Kate said there was someplace she had to go first. By now, the rain had stopped but everything was still wet. Kate got out of the car and hurried across the street and into the alleyway. She splashed through a puddle and then went down the black metal stairs that led to the black metal door with the slot. She knocked hard. For all she knew, the police had already been there and it was too late.

The slot slid open, and Tiffany looked out.

"What do you want?" she asked icily.

"To keep your boyfriend out of jail," Kate said.

Tiffany frowned.

"He doesn't have much time," Kate said, "so unless you're really into monthly conjugal visits, you'll let me talk to him right now."

The slot slid closed, leaving Kate wondering if Tiffany didn't believe her and was blowing her off. She was tempted to knock again, but had mixed feelings. How fitting would it be for Nick to get sent away knowing that it wouldn't have been that way if only Tiffany had let Kate speak to him. But even though Kate was certain it would turn Nick against Tiffany for good, she couldn't let that happen.

The slot opened, and this time Nick's eyes appeared. "I guess I don't have to ask what you're doing here."

"My dad turned state's evidence," Kate said. "And it turns out he's got plenty to say about your organization."

Nick blinked with astonishment.

"My guess is, you don't have much time," Kate said.

The slot closed. Kate could hear voices inside:

"What's going on?"

"The cops are going to be here any second."

"What do we do?"

"We go, fast."

The door opened, and Tiffany came out. She paused for a second and looked at Kate. "Why'd you tell him?"

"I guess I'm just a sucker for a nice guy," Kate replied.

Tiffany gave her a look like she was crazy, then hurried past her and up the steps. The door was open, and Kate poked her head in. The gambling joint was empty, and a door at the other end of the room was open. Kate heard the clang of metal, as if someone had slammed the door of a safe closed. A second later Nick came through the doorway with a satchel over his shoulder and hurried toward her.

"Lock the door behind you," Kate said.

"What's the point?" Nick asked.

"It'll make them think you're inside," Kate said. "They'll waste some time trying to break down the door."

Nick turned and locked the metal door. Then he and Kate went up the steps and through the alleyway. Once they got to the street, Nick headed toward his silver Mercedes.

"Don't," Kate said.

Nick stopped and scowled at her.

"The cops won't think you're here if your car isn't here," Kate said.

Nick stared at her, and a smile slowly crept across his lips. "You've always got it thought out, don't you?"

"Not always," Kate said, and waved him toward her car. "We'll take mine."

"Where to?" Nick asked as they got in.

"The bus station," Kate said. "It's more likely they'll look for you on a highway or at the airport."

Nick smirked. "And where am I going?"

"Wherever the first bus you can get on takes you," Kate said. "And if I were you, I'd just keep going." She glanced at the satchel now resting on Nick's lap. "Is that what I think it is?"

Nick nodded.

"Then you'll be okay for a while," Kate said.

"More than a while," Nick said. "I just have to get to the Cayman Islands and I'm good as gold."

A few moments later, Kate stopped in front of the bus station. Nick didn't move. "I don't know how I can thank you."

"Don't bother," Kate said.

He reached over and put his hand on hers. "There's a lot of money in that Cayman account. I mean millions. More than enough for both of us."

Kate smiled and drew her hand away from his. "Sorry."

Nick's face fell. "You sure?"

Kate gazed into his gorgeous blue eyes. She wasn't sure of

anything. Maybe she would just have to accept that it would be that way for a while.

"Go," she said. "But when you get settled, let me know where, okay?"

Nick smiled. He leaned over and kissed her quickly, then got out of the car. Kate watched as he went through the entrance to the bus station and vanished. She started to drive away, knowing she would go home and back to Teddy to see what might develop. Knowing also that her life, and her family's, would forever change now that the organization was no more. Where would they live? What would her father do? What would she do?

Kate glanced into the rearview mirror. The bus station was growing smaller, the distance between Nick and her growing greater. But she had a feeling that someday she would see him again.

What's life without a little . . .

DRAMA!

★ A new series by Paul Ruditis ★

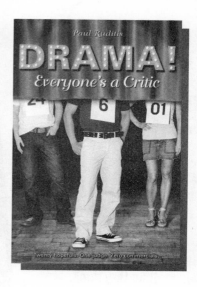

At Bryan Stark's posh private high school in Malibu, the teens are entitled, the boys are cute, and the school musicals are *extremely* elaborate. Bryan watches—and comments—as the action and intrigue unfold around him. Thrilling mysteries, comic relief, and epic sagas of friendship and love . . . It's all here. And it's showtime.

From Simon Pulse • Published by Simon & Schuster

In the beginning . . . there was a plan.
And the plan was good.

THE HACK:
Get a slacker into Harvard.

THE CREW:
Three nerds and a beauty queen.

THE PLAN:
Take down someone who deserves it.
Don't get distracted. Don't get caught.

THE STAKES:
A lot higher than they think.

HACKING HARVARD
by Robin Wasserman

- -

From **Simon Pulse**

Published by Simon & Schuster